COSMIC CATS

Cosmic Cats

ISBN 978-1-910779-07-1 (Paperback)

Produced and Typeset by
Oxford eBooks Ltd.

Oxford eBooks

An anthology of stories by children from
Mumias school, Kenya and
St Swithun's CE School, England

Contents

Introduction
By Paul Gamble

It has been a pleasure to play a small part in this book's journey, and to sense the creative energy that has led to the writing of these wonderful cat stories. Part of the joy has been the reminder that miles can shrink when stories are shared. What a treat to feel the force of such varied voices – and to know that many other children in Kenya and England wrote stories that aren't seen here. If only we'd had more space for you to be able to see all the tales of cat bravery and curiosity.

My good fortune was to see some of the St Swithun's writers hard at work as they crafted their stories. Their contribution to this book is the result of a special project, but it's worth pointing out that creative writing is a year-round activity in the school. Class teachers work hard at developing the many skills that feed into successful story-telling: use of clear descriptive language; a good story arc, with plot twists that keep the reader interested; a strong structure that leads to a satisfying ending; convincing use of direct speech – characters speaking (or miaowing) in ways that help them come to life. Giving young story-tellers the chance and the confidence to try out these things is what has allowed these stories to live and breathe. Congratulations to all St Swithun's teachers and writers!

But let's imagine for a moment the extra challenge of writing stories in a language other than the one you use in everyday life. Yes, that's the reality for those who wrote their stories in Kenya. I look back at my own childhood, long ago, and try to imagine how I and my classmates would have got on with a similar challenge. 'Not at all well' is the kindest answer I can suggest! So, I offer an especially loud round of applause and 'Congratulations!' to each of the successful Kenyan story-tellers. I hope you can hear me across the miles. Your stories are alive and well in faraway England. Many will read your words here. And they will feel that they know you, at least a little.

Allowing others to see or hear anything you've created requires a special ingredient: bravery. Every story told in these pages started as a blank sheet of paper. It grew out of one person's imagination, and started off on a journey whose end remains unknown. That's where each and every reader of the story comes in. You will find your own experience when you read the individual stories, recognising the familiar and learning some new things too.

As you read off the page or hear somebody else read the words (I'd really recommend the second of those), I'm confident you'll enjoy the journey. Remember what went into creating each story – the time, energy and care of the writer, the expertise and encouragement of teachers, the support given by adults at home and friends at school. Recognise the bravery of turning an empty page into a living story. And, perhaps above all, celebrate how story-telling has brought together children who live many miles apart.

Foreword
By Sylvia Vetta

The founder of the Nasio Trust Nancy Mudenyo Hunt and I wrote a novel together. *Not So Black and White* is about a courageous Kenyan girl determined to get an education and the affect she would have on young people in Kenya and in England. I suggested we give copies to the community libraries in west Kenya. Nancy pointed to a problem – there were none.

With some friends in the village of Kennington, we decided to raise money to build one. Our village had fundraised to build a spirulina production unit in Musanda so

we knew Nasio would deliver. We started to raise the money with concerts, open gardens and coffee mornings. The popular illustrator Korky Paul agreed to be our patron and spent a day in every class in St Swithun's school (Kennington). That contributed £1201.84 towards the building.

It would be delightful if the children of Mumias and the children of Kennington could have something to share. I believe that can be done through art and storytelling. I'm delighted that my granddaughters are avid readers. Without a love of reading and access to books in a library, I would not have had the life I've enjoyed. I certainly wouldn't have become an author. That is why I am passionate about every child having access to a library. Alexandra Vetta is an enthusiastic writer of stories. I suggested she write a story on the theme of CATS. Her sisters Antonia and Anastastia illustrated it and I sent copies to Mumias. A shortened version of Alexandra's story is printed at the end of the book.

The Kenyan children were asked to write on the same topic. It could be non-fiction, fiction or fantasy.

They did and it's amazing what they

achieved considering that English is not their first language. We asked the children of St Swithun's to do the same. Sadly we couldn't publish them all. The English Lead, Lesley Maskell, Classics teacher and Kennington Parish Councillor, Paul Gamble, and well known children's author Julia Golding had the difficult task of selecting the ones included in *Cosmic Cats*. The Nasio Trust and my aim was that it should be the first book in Mumias library so that the children know they belong there.

It is even more fun because Korky Paul has provided the cover illustration and Winnie the Witch's cat Wilbur has endorsed it. He also agreed to design the mural for the library using children of Mumias' art work with a contribution from St Swithun's.

I hope you enjoy it

Sylvia Vetta

Stories from Mumias Township Primary School

Mash the Cat

By Lilian Ajwang

Mash was a little cat that lived in a lighthouse. He helped the lighthouse keeper with his job of guiding ships safely.

One night there was a noisy storm raging. Lightning flashed and thunder rumbled. It was so loud that the cat couldn't sleep.

In the morning he looked outside. The stormy night had turned to a lovely sunny day. The sky was brilliant blue. But what was that noise? Someone was crying. Mash couldn't see who it was and scampered down the stairs to find out. When he reached the bottom of the lighthouse, it didn't take him long to find where the sound was coming from. Hiding in a pile of green seaweed was a baby seal.

"What's the matter?" he asked.

"I washed up here in the storm. I'm hungry and want to go home but I don't know where I am."

"What would a baby seal eat?"

Mash tried his own favourite food – cheese

but the seal refused to eat it. Mash returned to the kitchen and this time brought two fried fish. The baby seal was sleepy but when she ate the fish she became active and tried to jump up. After she ate the fish, she told Mash she wanted to go home. Mash called on a whale and asked

"Have you seen her mother?"

"No I am sorry I haven't but I'll help you look."

They rode on the back of the whale until they saw an albatross flying fast and high over the sea.

"Have you seen baby seal's mother?" they asked the albatross.

"I've seen ships and icebergs but I haven't seen the baby seal's mother. Ask turtle."

They soon found the turtle swimming nearby. He was sad to hear about the lost baby seal.

"I'm sorry I can't help. I missed the storm. I was in warmer seas hunting jelly fish. But I met some dolphins. You could ask them if they have seen baby seal's mother."

The day was drawing to a close. Mash was fed up. They had searched all day and he was tired. The baby seal started to cry again. As the sun began to set they sat on a buoy. Just then a friendly dolphin peeped his head out of the water.

"What's wrong?" he asked.

Dolphin suddenly looked happy. "I've seen baby seal's mother," he said.

Mash, whale and baby seal followed the dolphin back to the shore. There sitting on the rocks were a group of seals catching the last of the day's sunlight.

"Can you see your mother?" asked Mash.

Baby seal shook her head and began to cry.

Although baby seal had not seen her mother, her mother had seen her.

She raced over to give baby seal and Mash a big hug.

"Thank you for bringing my baby back. I've been so worried."

That night in the lighthouse, in his warm bed. Mash thought about baby seal and his mother. He had no trouble sleeping that night – no trouble at all.

Maisy's Cat
By Lodrine Aswani

Maisy loved cats. Cimm was a black cat with white stripes on his back. Cimm was a peaceful cat. Even if you accidentally stepped on her she would not harm you. Maisy prepared a delicacy for Cimm. She was happy to have a nice home and a friend like Maisy.

When Maisy went to school, Cimm waved a paw goodbye and when she returned home, she ran and jumped around her in a sign of welcome.

One day Maisy planned a picnic with Cimm. When they reached their destination, they ate their food and played. The sun was setting when Maisy packed up and looked around for

Cimm. She called out for her but Cimm was nowhere to be seen. Maisy returned home and was so worried she couldn't sleep. In the morning she went to the kitchen and there was Cimm fast asleep in her basket.

But there was something different. Sparks were flying from her body. In a thrash of a duck's tail Cimm was floating on air. Cimm's eyes shone like mirrors in the sun. Her eyes changed colour from blue to red to pink and yellow and back to green.

Maisy's mother fainted and Maisy was a bit scared to see her mother on the floor. Cimm came down, raised her tail and mewed three times and Maisy's mother woke up. Maisy's father left the house shouting "Miracle, Miracle!"

The neighbours arrived at Maisy's house and were amazed. One of them said,

"Cimm is a rainbow fairy magic pet." Maisy and her family liked the idea of having a rainbow fairy magic pet.

My Cat
By Michelle Amakore

I like my cat Mary because she likes playing with me.

It eats rice and drinks milk.

My friends like playing with Mary and watch her hunting in the flower garden.

Mary is black, brown and white.

Do you love her too?

A Pussy Cat with Grandmother

By Otoeno Bornface

One year ago, a pussy cat lived with my grandmother. They loved each other. The cat was so small that grandmother would carry it in her purse. Most days they would walk around the village and play chase.

One day the cat went with grandmother to the city to buy foodstuffs at the supermarket. When they reached their destination the cat saw a rat which looked very angry. Grandmother was busy and didn't notice. The cat decided to run after the rat. He chased it down the street until the cat became tired, stopped and looked around. He couldn't see the rat anywhere and couldn't remember where she had left grandmother.

Grandmother had become crazy looking for her cat. She started to cry so people came to see what was happening. All she kept saying was 'pussy'. Everyone wondered what she meant. Grandmother continued to cry until she fainted. She was rushed to the nearest hospital.

Meanwhile, the cat was looking for grandmother and also started crying. The cat had nowhere to go. After crawling for hours he met a big cat who decided to help him. He followed the big cat to his home for something to eat only to find that all there was to eat was the rat. He felt sorry for the rat, that they wanted to eat it. He was so tired he slept until the next day.

He found the supermarket but grandmother wasn't there, so he began the long walk back to the village. He found grandmother. She too had not eaten for two days because she was worried about her cat. When she saw her she was glad but also sad because the cat had become very thin. She brought food for him and the cat gobbled it up so quickly and greedily that she vomited on the floor. Grandmother was angry and put the cat in a sack and put him outside.

 A bad thing happened. The cat died in the sack and grandmother was full of regret and sorrow.

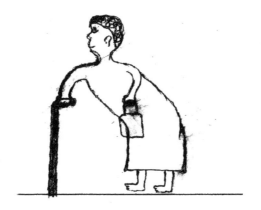

Precious the Cat
By Limdali Alliambo

My cat is called Precious. She is a good cat and is black, red and yellow. She likes to eat meat and fish. My cat likes to sleep with me in my bed.

I like to play football with my cat.

But my cat is not friendly to rats. Today she caught a rat and brought it to me. She thinks she is a hero so I gave her milk and a cake.

The Cat Determined to Board a Plane

By Olouch Joseph Odhiambo

The cat Fantasa was born in Brazil. Fantasa was a male cat that was given a female name after his mother who died in labour and his father died of stress.

Fantasa was lonely until the cat met Gregory, a monk in one of Brazil's sacred places. Fantasa loved Gregory who provided him with all he needed.

Living in the church with the monks, Fantasa heard stories of how black people from Africa came to Brazil. One morning, sitting alone in the church yard, he saw a brightly coloured light moving in the high heavens. The thing landed on the ground and took ten minutes to slow down to a stop. The thing looked like a toy that Gregory had given him – a toy plane.

Fantasa said "Meow Meow" as he pointed to the plane. Gregory smiled, picked him up and put Fantasia on his shoulder. Fantasa wanted to explore the plane but Gregory had come to welcome visitors.

During the celebrations with the visitors, Fantasa joined in the dancing and loved eating sausages.

He woke early in the morning. Gregory did not pray for long before carrying Fantasa to where the plane was parked. The door was open and both entered the plane.

At first Fantasa thought this was a nightmare come true. Then Gregory fastened the seat belt. Hours later Fantasa looked out of the window and viewed London below.

Tashs' Cat Adi

By Delvine Krisiangani

Tashs bought all the items that her mother sent her to buy in the supermarket. On the way back home she came across a cat. The cat seemed hungry. His blue eyes shone as Tashs looked at him. She gave the cat some milk and said,

"What is your name and where are you from?"

"My name is Adi. I have never found favour from any human. I am happy to have your favour." The cat truly liked Tashs and she did not find it difficult to like him back.

Evening arrived and darkness began to cover the earth. Adi walked out into the garden. Adi saw Tashs and ran towards her.

That night Tashs woke up.

A noise was coming from the storeroom. This was unusual. She picked up a lamp and courageously walked towards it. She opened the door to find Adi eating a mouse.

The mouse's family wondered how they could get rid of Adi. They put out some milk and added a sleeping powder. They waited while Adi drank the milk and began to doze. They rushed towards him and put a bell around the cat's neck so now the mouse family could hear the cat coming.

The Cat from the Black Mountains

By Newton Okutoyi

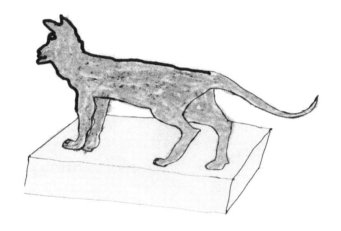

Sarah was going past the King's palace when she saw a stone cat.

It stood on a stone slab just inside the gates, it had big brown eyes.

"It looks like it could come alive any minute," whispered Sarah.

"Yes," said someone standing behind her.

She turned to see a boy with black hair dark eyes. He was wearing a blue tunic.

She had never seen him before so asked him where he was from.

"I come from the Black Mountains. It was alive. The King's magician turned it to stone and brought it here."

"How do you know?" asked Sarah.

"I come from the Black Mountains. It was my friend."

"But..." began Sarah

"Move away from the gates. The King will soon be coming!" shouted the King's guard.

She turned around but the boy was gone

Sarah told her grandmother what she had seen and what the boy had told her. She told her that on the following day they ought to try to see the King.

She went to bed thinking about the blue stone cat. That night she slept in the strange old bed her grandmother called the bed of dreams. Strange things happened to Sarah whenever she slept in the bed of dreams.

She woke in the middle of the night and saw a fox standing at the bottom of her bed. Its eyes shone in the moonlight. The fox told her to go and meet Tristan.

"Who is Tristan?" she asked.

He's the boy you met yesterday.

Sarah climbed out of bed and looked out of the window

The stars were out and the moon was shining. She saw someone in the shadow of a tree.

She threw her shawl over her shoulders.

"This way," said the fox.

He led the way outside. A boy stepped into the moonlight. He had a rope ladder over his shoulders.

"Here is Sarah," said the fox. "She will set the great cat free."

"I must take him back to the Black Mountains. You must cross the silver river, wash your hands in the water, then stroke the cat seven times to break the magician's spell. The Magician has set a spell on the river so that I cannot cross it but you can," Tristan explained

"Of course I will," she said.

They followed a stream that led to the river. There was a little waterfall. She held her hands out to touch the water and they shone like silver in the moonlight. Tristan waited for her on the other side of the bridge.

They ran through the dark streets to the palace. Tristan tied the rope to a tree and hung it over the wall. He helped Sarah climb over.

She rubbed the cat seven times and waited.

The cat came to life. And Tristan took him back to the Black Mountains
  This is how Sarah and Tristan saved the cat from the Black Mountains.

A Cat

By Marion A Dari

My cat is funny and plays up and down the house. He will even jump over the wall into the street and he loves to climb trees.

I call him Teddy.

Teddy also likes to spend time in the chair.

When he sees me put out his milk, he jumps up and comes to me.

I love my cat but some of my neighbours hate Teddy. One day my friend Lucy said that Teddy had eaten food they had poisoned and he had died. I rushed to see but it wasn't Teddy. It was another cat

Sometimes Teddy even makes me angry. I left a stew to cook but he jumped up and ate it.

Beky the Cat

By Jacintah Auma

It was Rosy's birthday. She woke up early. She went to the bathroom and then put on her beautiful, short, yellow dress. When Rosy went outside she was surprised to see flowers and balloons and her best friends.

Everything was ready for her birthday party. Everyone gave Rosy a gift. One friend gave Rosy a small black cat. Rosy was happy and named her Beky.

She found a big box for Beky. When Rosy came home from school she went to the cupboard where her mother kept the milk but it was all gone. Beky had drunk it! Rosy was not happy. After that Rosy told Beky to hunt in the forest for rats.

From that day on, when Becky felt hungry she went in the forest in search of food.

About Cats

By Ezzine Chiriswa

A cat is a small domestic animal that eats rats. I like playing with cats. My favourite cat is called Miriam.

One day on my way to school I left my cat at home. When I came, I put my school bag down and looked for Miriam but I couldn't find her. I was very sad.

Then he came out of the forest looking very hungry. I gave him some milk. I went to the market and bought some string.

From then on, when I went to school, I put a long string on him so he would be safe until

I came home.

Joel's favourite animal was a dog. Everywhere he went he admired the dogs he met. How he longed to have one as a pet.

On New Year's Day morning he went downstairs to find his Mum and Dad sitting on the couch. He greeted them on his way to take tea in the dining room. After tea Joel's Mum called out "Joel".

And guess what? From behind the couch a lovely pet dog came out. Joel had what he'd always longed for.

My Cat

By Michel Auma

My favourite animal is a cat and my cat is black and white. Every day I give my cat milk so it can be healthy like me.

My cat likes to eat meat and fish. But my cat is a hunter and eats rats too.

When it hunts in the garden its eyes shine like a star.

I love my cat so much.

Cat

By Violet Khaswa

Cats are found in most of the world. I have a pet cat called Katty. I love the sound of the soft pads of her feet. She walks without making hardly a sound.

I love Katty because she is one of the cutest cats. She is intelligent and uses her litter box so doesn't make the house dirty.

She likes sitting in the window watching the outside world. When she is hungry she sits by her dish signalling to me to give her food.

Katty's favourite food is boiled fish and the smell of it makes her run around and wag her tail in a crazy way.

The peculiar thing about Katty is that she likes to watch TV especially the Animal Planet channel. She is not just my pet but a family member.

Research says that petting cat reduces the chance of a heart attack because it relieves stress. Katty helps me when I feel lonely.

Messi the Cat

By Yusuf

It was Christmas morning. I went downstairs and found my mother by the Christmas tree. She called to me, "Honey, open this box."

Inside was a black and white cat with a red mouth and beautiful eyes. I named him Messi because Messi is my favourite football player.

That night, I fell asleep with Messi beside me.

One day I went to church. When we were finished praying and I returned home I couldn't find Messi. I made posters saying, 'Have you seen my cat? Messi is missing.'

I put posters up all over town but no one had seen him. I searched and searched. When I saw him under a tree, I ran towards him like lightning. I couldn't believe my eyes. Messi had given birth to a group of kittens.

Messi was a girl!

Old Mother Cat

By John Odhiambo

There was once an old mother cat which lived in a hollow tree. The cat was blessed to give birth to a litter of kittens. They were so beautiful that they made her proud.

One day a girl named Vanilla passed by. Vanilla was eleven and learned in the Upper School near her home. She heard the kittens meowing and moved closer. She was delighted on seeing the beautiful litter. An idea struck her. She chose a brown kitten with white spots. It had been her dream since she was seven years old to have a kitten.

Her parents said 'yes' because some mice had destroyed some important documents and they hoped the kitten would get rid of the mice.

Vanilla had an elder brother called Sebastian. Together built a house for the kitten and Sebastian went to buy Kata food.

The cat needed a name, so Vanilla called it Biden. As she grew Biden played games with Vanilla and sometimes she jumped on the table where Vanilla studied and began meowing.

45

Vanilla was distracted so she carried Biden to her bicycle and cycled with her around the town. When it came to her exams Vanilla's results were poor and her parents blamed Biden. They made Vanilla study in her room with the door shut so that Biden could not disturb her.

The kitten sat in the doorway waiting for Vanilla. It felt lonely, bored and sad. Biden got thinner and thinner as the days went by.

Late one evening when everyone was asleep, Biden saw a mouse in the house. He chased it and jumped out of the window. There he saw another cat and they went off together in the starry night. Vanilla and her family never saw Biden again.

Hunter's Cat

By Sharipher Eshesa

Some of Hunter's neighbours talked about witchcraft because his home was full of cats.

One cloudy day, he found a cat beside the road. It had been hit by a car and was in a bad condition.

"Oh what a beautiful cat," said Hunter.

He gave the cat some water but it had difficulties breathing, so he pumped some air in it. He covered it with a small towel and carried him home. He gave it milk until the sick cat became strong and healthy.

One day Hunter bought meat for his wife to cook. When she came home, she was angry because the cat had jumped on the table and eaten their meat. She shouted angrily at the cat and it ran away and never came back.

The man was called Hunter because he was a hunter. Every morning he went hunting. One day he saw the cat playing with butterflies. It followed him and looked happy when Hunter welcomed him back in his home.

Shopping
By Saida

Melvin went to the shop one morning. Outside the shop was an old brown cat. She asked the shopkeeper to give her some milk to feed the cat. But the shopkeeper told her "Get out and don't come back."

Melvin went home with tears on her face. She walked slowly towards the house. And went to her room and cried.

On her way home from school on Monday evening, she found a kitten in the long grass and went towards it. She carried the pretty cat home and named it Tom.

The Christmas Present
By Aponga Rujab

Some people thought that Rajab was obsessed with cats. She had it all. Cat posters, cat cushions and even a cat duvet. All that was missing was a cat. How she longed for one. It was all she talked about.

So imagine her delight when one Christmas morning she went downstairs in her Christmas PJs to find a box beneath the Christmas tree. She began to tear at the present.

"Slow down, Rajab," chuckled her father.

"This is exactly what I wanted," said Rajab. She hugged the toy cat in delight.

"How about you open the next one?" said her Mum as she pushed a green parcel towards her. It contained cat food, a cat bed and cat toys.

Rajab gasped "You don't mean..."

Her parents gently pushed a big blue box. Inside was a black cat with turquoise eyes and a bright pink nose. She lifted up the kitten with shaky hands and it licked her on the nose. Her eyes filled with happy tears as she looked at her parents.

"I love him so much." The two became inseparable.

Moving House

By Stephen Mushieni

The cat was playing in the sun. It stopped and said "Today is moving day. I'm going to find myself a new house."

She packed up her blanket and pillow and her books.

Very soon she found a little house. She peeked in through the door and looked around.

"This is a perfect house," cried the cat.

It was my house and I made it welcome and gave it milk.

51

Missing Bony and Popa
By Rahma Keya

Popa took good care of her kittens Bang and Pop, so they grew healthy and big. When the kittens were old enough to hunt for themselves, she taught them how to hunt.

She led them to the nearby forest. Suddenly a rat appeared and Popa jumped and grabbed it. She killed it and fed it to the kittens.

"Next time I will let you go alone to hunt," she told her kittens.

The kittens woke early the next morning and set out for the forest. When Popa woke, her kittens were missing. She went out looking for them calling "Meow" but she didn't find them. So went back home hoping they were there. She called again but there was no answer and this made Popa even more worried.

She thought they would be afraid of the dark night but in the morning, they had still not come home. When she called "meow, meow", a passing hyena laughed at her. She thought her kittens were gone forever. She went looking expecting to find their bodies.

52

Then she saw Bang and Pop running towards her.

"Where have you been?" she asked them.

"Mamma this man took us to his home."

Popa looked at the man angrily.

Bang said, "Mama he gave us food and milk."

"And the food was so sweet," added Pop. They all decided to become friends with, and live with the man.

The Cat Mirror

By Linda Keya

I have two cats. One is called Peter Parker and the other Chitti. Peter Parker is a male cat and Chitti is female. They are both brown and white. Chitty is the most playful. She likes dancing with rope and string. One day Chitti followed me into my bedroom.

She went towards my wall mirror. When she saw her image in the mirror she crouched down and clawed at the mirror with her paws. I didn't understand why she did that and wondered if she thought the cat in the mirror was another cat.

My cats watch TV with me and my siblings. They like *Tom and Jerry*. But Chitti and Peter Parker do not fight. They are always good friends and Peter protected Chitty when a wild dog tried to hurt her.

I pray for them so that God can protect them.

The cat in the Tree

By Laurence Atsulu

I like playing with my cat and my cat also likes playing with my friend Jet.

In the afternoon we went with Jet to his house for tea. On the way a dog jumped out and barked. When my cat heard the sound, he ran away but I think the dog wanted to play with my cat.

My cat climbs up in the tree because he likes to eat fruit.

My cat goes with me to fetch water.

Lost Cat

By Nusra Amekecho

Once upon a time lived a girl called Jane. Her favourite animal was a cat, so she asked her parents if she could have one.

One day her parents surprised her by giving her a male cat which she named Tom. She fed her cat and even slept with him.

When her school opened after the holiday Jane was sad to leave Tom. When her mother went to the shop, she did not close the door tightly. When Jane came home from school she went to play with Tom but couldn't find him.

The next day was Saturday so Jane went to look for her cat. She saw one by the side of the road and followed it. The cat stopped and looked at her

"What's your name?" asked Jane.

"John," was the reply.

"What a wonderful name you have," said Jane.

Just then she saw Tom coming towards her. Tom cuddled up to her

She took Tom and John back home. Now

when she went to school she was not worried because Tom and John were friends. They played together and were never lonely.

Stories From St Swithun's

The Upside Down Cat
By Ikram

One nice and sunny day there was a cat called Bunnty. He woke up and felt very dizzy so he went back to sleep. When he woke up again he still felt dizzy.

So he said to himself "Why not I go to my friends house?" But when he came out of his bed he felt that something was wrong but he said "No, nothing is wrong." But what he was doing wrong was a handstand. He even wore his clothes the wrong way without noticing in the mirror.

Bunnty even forgot to lock the door before going to his friends house. When Bunnty arrived to his friends house, instead of putting his shoes in the shoe rack, he put it in the bin.

When he put his shoes in the bin he went upstairs and fell asleep in his friends soft and cosy bed.

Leo the cat wakes up his friend Bunnty and He says "It is time to have lunch." But instead of having his usual food Tuna Fish, Bunnty went in the garden and caught the lonely and sad squirrel and ate it for his lunch in one go.

His friend Leo is confused because Bunnty is doing everything the wrong way and the opposite of the things that he is supposed to do.

So Leo thought "Why not I go to my lab and try and make a medicine for Bunnty." The medicine that Leo the cat was making for Bunnty was called The Bunnty medicine because it is only for Bunnty.

Leo was nervous because Bunnty does not like medicines. Leo had to wait until Bunnty falls asleep. Leo watched Bunnty carefully going upstairs.

After a while Bunnty fell asleep and was snoring and this was Leo's last chance to put the medicine in Bunnty's mouth.

The medicine went gushing down his mouth then suddenly Bunnty woke up and felt much better. Bunnty was back to normal again and also the alive squirrel popped out of his mouth and bit Bunnty's hand.

Bunnty and Leo was surprised because Squirrel was doing the same thing that Bunnty was doing. The squirrel was putting his clothes on the wrong way. He even put his socks on his hands. And Leo said "Oh no, not again, do I have to make another medicine?"

Cats In Charge
By Sebastian

Chapter 1 – The Prank

Once Ben was thinking of what happened yesterday, and he explained it to his Mum. Here is what happened. Ben was at Cat School and saw his friends Tom, Jack, Albert and Wilf. They started a conversation of what pranks they could do on Miss Claws today.

They snuck into Miss Claws' classroom and saw her watching television about how to lick yourself more efficiently and cook tuna in a better way.

Tom said "Why would you want to make

tuna better because I don't even like tuna?!" But they watched the television and found out.

Then they put string outside the door which they thought she would trip over, and slip onto the floor that was recently mopped. When Miss Claws decided to walk out, she slipped over head first and did the splits! Tom, Ben, Jack, Albert and Wilf all laughed for about an hour.

Miss Claws thought of a very good plan to get her own back and prank on the boys. Miss Claws knew very well it was the boys as this had happened a load of times. She had never got her own back but she thought today is the day she would get her own back.

Miss Claws' plan was very sneaky – to go to the boys' houses and do something mischievous in there.

Chapter 2 – The Robbery

Miss Claws snuck into Ben's house first, but ended up backing off because she saw a robber already stealing! Miss Claws instantly took a picture of the robber and the Police took the robber away. The robber's name was Mr Dinkledun Whiskers.

Miss Claws went to all the other boys' houses and managed to do her plan with them. And here's what she did. She went into all their houses and stole all of their sword fighting certificates. In the morning all the boys started going a bit crazy because they had spent a lot of effort on those. The next day they earned another award at the Cat Sword Fighting School.

Chapter 3 – The Secret Forest

When Miss Claws got to her office, a pipe came from the ceiling and sucked everything up including herself. She ended up in a strange forest with black wood and magenta leaves.

She leaned back against one of the trees, and she seemed to activate something but she didn't know what. Suddenly, a massive elevator dropped onto the ground with a big bang! She stepped on, and it started flinging her up until she got to the clouds. Then she banged down onto a tree, and she found this secret machine.

Meanwhile, the boys were at Cat School watching television, because the teacher wasn't there. When they finally thought that Miss Claws was gone, the same pipe that sucked up Miss Claws appeared right where they were! Everything and everyone else in the whole Cat School was sent into the secret forest. But what they didn't know was that this forest contained a lot more than it looked like.

One boy was the first to discover that this thing had secrets. He fell into a massive pit hole that wasn't really massive.

Chapter 4 – The Endless Field

When they got out of the mysterious forest, they were in a field... but not any type of field, an endless field. It had a lot of different things in it, mainly cards of different cats which had been very famous. They went deeper into the field and saw a lot of things they had never seen before, like a floating house, a never moving cloud and a door on its own.

Then they went back into the forest and saw Miss Claws moaning quite a lot louder than they did. She was saying "Oh I wish I was home! This is such an endless forest and field!" Miss Claws wailed. The boys were looking for any way they could get back, but couldn't find anything at all except for a trash can, a bag of toffee apples and an old sock.

They decided to make them into a pipe shape to try to get out like the pipe that brought them in. But the pipe led to nothing but a stinky smell.

Chapter 5 – Home

They went back to the elevator, which jumped in a perfect angle just onto the clouds. They found this mysterious portal, but they had to jump onto other clouds while falling to get to the portal. They jumped and they jumped and they jumped until they got to the portal. It took them back to the Cat School in time for lunch.

After lunch, they had a really good break time in the mud. Miss Claws was laying down in her office, really tired and covered in bruises. Finally, when Miss Claws got up, it was the end of lunch.

Chapter 6 – The New President

The next day, there was a new vote for the President, and one of the people you could vote for wasn't really a person – because they were a cat. The cat was called Migrim Loner. She wanted to be a president for all the Cat-tacular things she could do. The other four people you could vote for were actual people.

The cat won because nearly all the children and every cat voted for Migrim Loner. Loner of course, won, but she was only 1 point ahead of another contestant. When she was the President, the only thing on TV was cooking shows about anchovies and the best way to catch anchovies. The President loved anchovies so much because they made her so smart.

Ben, Albert, Tom, Jack and Wilf all had a very nice life, because the President was really kind.

The Magic Cat
by Zoya

One hot summer day, a girl was walking through a park. The girl was called Lily. She had ginger hair and wore pink earrings.

Lily spotted a boy crying and wanted to do something about it. She asked him what was wrong.

"Why are you crying?"

"I'm crying because my older brother hit me and I got hurt," answered the boy

"Why did he hit you?"

"Because I was saying something rude to him."

"But that's not a reason to hit someone," said Lily.

"Wait a minute. I can see that your knee is hurt. I'll bring something cold."

Lily went to buy a bag of frozen peas. She took it to the boy.

"Here you go. I hope this will help and you must talk to your brother and Mum about what he did."

"Thank you. You are very kind," replied the

boy.

Lily went out to play. She heard weird cat-like sounds coming from the garage. She went in and found a cat shape floating in the air like a big cloud. She walked towards it and all of a sudden the cloud sucked her in. Lily was frightened and closed her eyes.

When she opened her eyes, she was on a flying mattress with wings. She looked for somewhere to land. She looked around and she could see shells, sand and the ocean.

Then she spotted something in the distance, padding its way towards her. It looked like a cat but no ordinary cat.

The cat could talk.

"You were kind to that boy, Lily so I wanted you to enjoy some magic."

Cats vs Cat Killers

By Bulsie

On a lovely day in England, there were four little stray kittens and a strange, cute stray puppy. There was:

Lucky

Bill

Kit

Liz

And Fluffy the Dog

The five of them were playing on a hill full of shiny, green, grass sparkling in the sunrise.

All of a sudden Fluffy jumped on Liz, grabbed her and bit into her soft fluffy skin!

"Oi," cried Liz. Fluffy growled and sprinted towards Bill. Bill screamed and tried to run but he tripped, lost his balance and fell to the ground! Fluffy leaned over him and bit him. He squeaked and tried to stand up, but the bite was too painful, so he couldn't. Bill shouted to Kit and Liz. Fluffy looked at Kit and picked her out for his next victim.

He charged at her, jumped and took her down.

At the same time in the faraway land called America, in Los Angeles, in a glamorous office a man was sitting at his walnut desk. His name was Fletcher Bowron. Dressed in a silk suit, he was working on his secret project. He developed a special machine that could control dogs and make them cruel and evil cat killers. As a result everyone would put their dogs in shelters and become cat owners. He adored cats and loathed dogs, because when he was a baby, a dog bit him on the eye and he lost his eyesight and had a traumatic surgery that he could never forget.

Fluffy was the special machine's first victim. Fletcher was extremely satisfied with the result of the machine. He was working on a stronger and faster signal to spread the cruelty and evilness across the world.

Back In England Fluffy ran down the hill to kill or hurt more cats. When he disappeared in the distance Bill, Kit and Liz painfully stood up and ran to the trash can that was their home. The lid was removed the trash can was turned up-side down and a stick was holding it. There were three trash cans turned to their sides joind together with a bit of metal and some tape. There were also some blankets.

The kittens drank some water from the clean and shiny pond.

"Come on guys we need to get Fluffy before he gets too far," cried kit. They jumped up and raced after Fluffy.

"I can't see him," explained Liz.

"He couldn't get that far!" murmured Bill. They ran across the big, warm hill. The four kittens ran across Bagley Wood Road until they reached Waitrose a big shop in Abingdon.

"There he is!" shouted Liz. The four kittens looked in the direction Liz was pointing to. There was a dog that looked like Fluffy, it was running away.

"Lets get him," cried Kit. They charged at the dog. The dog turned around and growled at them. He started to charge at them but suddenly he paused, he blinked and jumped on them but this was a nice hug not a painful bite.

Flecher was furious he couldn't believe that his machine didn't work. Back in England Lucky, Bill, Kit, Liz and Fluffy were talking...

"What were you doing just then?" asked Liz?

"What do you mean? I was playing with you on the big hill how we usually do," replied Fluffy.

"We didn't play, you bit us instead of playing with us," said Bill.

All of a sudden three lights flashed past them. The friends turned around and saw three strong muscly dogs. The dogs growled and charged at them. When they got close they jumped on the kittens.

"Auuu!!!!!" cried Kit. Fluffy quickly jumped on the attackers. He sunk his teeth into their skin wherever he reached them. The three attackers ran away. Liz quickly looked at the dog's badges.

"They're from Los Angeles," cried Liz.

"Off we go to Los Angeles!" exclaimed Fluffy. The others giggled. They ran across Abingdon and they hopped on a bus to the beach! When they reached the beach they jumped on a large ship that was going to Los Angeles.

One day later, they were in Los Angeles.

They ran across some markets and into the mayor's building! They ran upstairs to Bowron Flecher's room and BANGED open the door. Sitting behind an expensive shiny desk was the evil Fletcher Bowron's cruel face. The four kittens jumped on him whilst Fluffy jumped on his desk and grabbed his special machine and threw it on the floor. It made a loud noise, exploded and disappeared.

A short time later, a servant came in to check the noise. When he saw the kittens holding Fletcher on the floor, he asked Fluffy what happened and Fluffy acted it out. The servant understood and called the police. Fletcher was taken to jail and all the dogs in the world became free again.

Fluffy's Dancing Adventure

By Susan

One rainy day, Fluffy gets a letter from her family who live far away. Her family were dancing cats and she wished she could dance with them. Fluffy was a cat who loved exploring and she had left her family to have her adventures. Fluffy had enjoyed her time travelling, but the letter made her feel homesick. She missed her family, especially her mum and dad.

She felt lonely, so she decided to watch television. In between her favourite dancing programmes, there was an advert for a dance competition. The prize was to have a free trip anywhere in the world, a trophy, and some shiny, golden tap-dancing shoes. This gave Fluffy an idea, if she won the competition, she could return home to see her family. She wanted to show them her skills and to dance with them. The competition was the day after next.

Fluffy rushed to her suitcase and took out her old dancing shoes. They were black and dusty and were a bit small for her paws. She put on her shoes and practiced the dances she learned when she was a kitten. She practiced to the music on the radio all day and all night. She picked her favourite song, it was called 'The Dancing Kittens'. It was a happy tune but very fast so there of lots of moves to learn.

There was one problem, Fluffy was very forgetful. When she sees a dog, she forgets they like to chase her. When she went to a fancy-dress party, she forgot her costume. She even forgot her own birthday! Fluffy was worried she would forget her moves on competition day. She was so worried, she packed her bag and then had one last practice before sleeping.

The day had arrived! Fluffy was so excited

she didn't stop to have her usual mouse for breakfast. She picked up her bag and rushed out to the bus station. She didn't want to be late.

She arrived early, but Fluffy didn't mind because she wanted time to practice.

"I finally remembered everything and I'm even here early!" she said excitedly. She took out her music and tried to find her shoes. She kept looking, and looking, but her shoes weren't there.

"Arghhh!" she meowed, "I must have forgotten to put them in my bag last night. I was so excited I didn't check this morning."

Fluffy started to cry because if she lost the competition, she wouldn't get to see her family or dance with them. Fluffy started to panic but looking for the shoes had taken so much time; the competition had started. What could she do?

She tried to dance without any shoes, but her paws were so fluffy, they didn't make a sound. How could she tap dance without making a tapping noise? She needed to find or make some new shoes quickly.

She tried to tie wooden spoons to her paws. They made a noise, but it wasn't loud enough.

People at the back of the studio would not hear her dance. Fluffy was scared, she didn't know what to try next.

She looked around and tried to find something else to use. Fluffy found some bells and tied them to her paws. They made a very loud noisel Too loud a noise! She heard them call out it was her turn next... Fluffy was getting very worried.

She searched around the back of the stage. She needed something metal like the bells, but which didn't jingle. Fluffy looked and looked. She even looked in the bin! Inside the bin she found some empty cans and elastic bands.

She heard someone say "Fluffy, it's your turn now." She squashed the cans and held them in place with the elastic bands. She walked onto the stage nervously.

The music started and she began to dance. As she did, the cans squashed even more. Fluffy felt silly, her family would never dance on cans. But it did make the right noise! It was a tapping noise. She looked at the audience to see if they liked it.

At first, everyone was silent, then suddenly the crowd went wild. They loved it. As they clapped, she danced faster and faster and she felt fantastic. Fluffy was amazed the cans worked! When the music stopped, she curtseyed. She felt proud and wished her family had seen her.

She was the last to dance and the scores came next. The judge announced the top three dancers.

"In third place is Ballerina Ben... in second place is Break-Dancing Frankie... and the winner is.... Fluffy, the amazing tin-can dancing cat!"

Fluffy couldn't believe it.

She shouted "Hooray, I've won!"

She was given the trophy, the ticket to go anywhere in the world – and of course some shiny golden tap-dancing shoes. Fluffy was so excited, now she could go and stay with her family, and dance with them in her new gold sparkly tap-dancing shoes. Her dream had come true!!

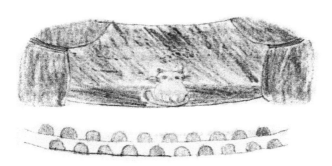

A Cat Called Chippy
By Hazel

There was once a cat called Chippy. She wasn't any old cat but a COOL cat! She could use a beat box and play electric guitar and much more that I can't remember.

She was nice but could be tough sometimes. I know she might look cute but she didn't act it! So she could be a bit naughty! She was very sassy sometimes, So that made her act like a Queen. It made her think she was the best and most important cat. And she'd do anything for fame (or a treat)! She had some friends as well called Mippy, Jippy, Hippy and Bippy.

Now, on with the story. One day Chippy was still busy playing her solo on the electric guitar.

When she'd finally finished, Jippy said: "That was one long solo!"

"Sorry," said Chippy, "I just got distracted". By the way, they were practising for a concert the following weekend.

So Chippy put her electric guitar down and turned to have a discussion with her band.

And when they had finished, she turned round to pick up her guitar, but it had disappeared.

"Hey, where did my guitar go?" she called.

"Yeah, my drums too!" moaned Mippy.

And ALL of the other instruments were gone … they searched and searched, but there was no sign of them.

"You know what we have to do then?" said Kippy.

"Yep", said the others. So they went onto the stage and transformed their clothing into Superhero costumes ready to save their instruments. Their ears turned purple and so did their flexible tails. Chippy's fur took on a reddish tint. She leaped around sniffing to see who had stolen the kittens' instruments.

"It's THIS way," she mewed.

So they leapt over onto a rock. And then into a deep hole.

"Oh well!" said Bippy.

"Let's go," Kippy panted. So they slunk through the tunnel, but came across a place where it split into different directions. They sniffed the air and all pointed in the same direction.

"It's THAT way!" They nodded and ran through the tunnel which led to a lair.

And there in front of Chippy's very eyes was a RAT.

"I am a Lab Rat," the rat said.

"Well, why did you steal our instruments?" Chippy fumed. She could smell lotions and potions and chemicals all over the burrow.

"So that's what I could smell outside!" said Chippy. She and the other cats had just remembered what Lab Rat was.

"A rat, a RAT!" they shouted, and chased it all around his burrow.

"I can't run any faster!" Lab Rat puffed, "Have the instruments back..."

"Why did you want them anyway?" asked Kippy curiously.

"I just wanted to use them for my music machine," the Lab Rat said, holding his tail nervously.

"OK" said the cats looking back.

"Bye then," said Lab Rat, as the kittens disappeared back down the tunnel.

On Saturday they performed their concert so well that they became famous and Chippy's solo was not quite so long.

Destiny and Mittens the Magical Cat

By Martha

Chapter 1

The rain hammered on the window as loud as elephants marching, and 10-year old Destiny looked out on the sea of skyscrapers across wet London with her chin in her hand and her face looking sad.

Destiny lived on the 15th floor of a massive block of flats. She lived there with her Mum, her Dad and her older brother Henry who was always very unkind to her. Their flat was small for all of them and it didn't have a garden, but Destiny loved the outdoors and nature more than anything in the world. Just down the road from her flat there was a little park and Destiny tried to visit it every day so she could be close to nature and feel free from her cramped flat, and her mean brother. She wasn't allowed to go there on her own and on the wet days it was more difficult for her to go to the park because her parents never wanted to take her in the rain.

"What a shame it's raining," said Henry sarcastically "it means you can't go to your precious park today."

"Just be quiet," Destiny said rolling her eyes.

"You're never going to escape your family, you know. You're stuck here forever!" said Henry, laughing as he walked away.

A fire of anger grew in Destiny's tummy and suddenly she realised she had to get out. While her parents and her brother were in the other room, she tiptoed past. When she got to the front door, she ran. As soon as she got outside, she felt free like a bird flying in the breeze. Destiny had run straight to the little park down the road and when she got there she stopped and breathed in the fresh air and spun around with her arms stretched out enjoying the space around her.

Destiny sat on her favourite bench near the fountain and suddenly out of the corner of her eye she saw a black and silver flash whizz past her. She rubbed her eyes and looked again. There was nothing there, but then she felt something rubbing against her leg.

Chapter 2

Destiny was petrified and very slowly looked down to see what was brushing her leg. On the wet ground by her feet there was the smallest of little kittens. Destiny was so relieved that it wasn't anything scary but she couldn't believe her eyes. The little kitten was really cute with greenish-blue eyes, a silver tummy, a black body, a long tail and silver paws.

"You gave me a fright, little kitty!" said Destiny. The kitten looked at her with her big, beautiful eyes.

"Where do you live and where is your family?" asked Destiny. The kitten looked down and looked sad.

"Maybe you don't have a family?" And the kitten meowed. Destiny felt sad for the little cat, but the kitten rolled onto its back playfully and for the rest of the evening Destiny played with the kitten and had so much fun.

Hours passed and Destiny realised that it was getting late and she had to go home.

"I have to go now, but I'd like to play with you again. I'll be back soon." And then Destiny ran all the way home and sneaked in the front door hoping her parents or her brother wouldn't notice her coming in. The first thing she saw when she turned from the front door was her mother standing with her hands on her hips.

"Where were you. Destiny?" her mother said looking angry and worried.

"I, I, I, I went litter picking around the flats..." replied Destiny nervously.

"OK..." said her mother in an unconvinced voice. "I really hope you didn't go further, you know how I don't like you going out on your own."

"No Mum, I'd never do that," said Destiny looking down as she told a lie.

Her Mum walked to the kitchen to make the supper and Destiny let out an enormous sigh of relief. Just then her brother Henry appeared out of nowhere.

"Litter picking? Really? I can't believe she fell for it. I know you went to the park, but I won't tell on you if you do my chores for a month. Oh, and my homework too."

Destiny wanted to scream in her brother's face, but she knew she had no choice and she had to do what he said. She was really excited to get back to the park to see her new friend again. She'd never had a pet before and maybe the kitten could become her pet.

"OK, deal. But you promise you won't tell?" said Destiny

"Promise," said Henry, and then he said "for now..." under his breath.

Chapter 3

The next day, Destiny was sat in her room doing Henry's history homework when her Mum shouted...

"I'm just popping to the shops!"

Destiny heard her Mum's car engine roaring like a tiger and the sound of the car driving away. She peered out of her bedroom and saw Henry sitting on the sofa glued to his computer games.

"Henry?" But he didn't answer. She walked past him and he didn't move. Destiny quietly crept towards the front door and as quick as a flash she ran out of the door.

As soon as she got to the park she felt she could breathe. She went to the bench and looked all around, but there was no sign of the cat. For a moment, Destiny panicked but then she heard a little squeak. And there, under the bench was the little cat.

"There you are! I'm so pleased to see you. I should really give you a name... let's see... Tibby? No. Lucky? Hmm, not right. How about Mittens because of your silver paws." And the little cat meowed.

Just then, Destiny noticed something.

"Hey Mittens, how come you're so wet?" asked Destiny "it's not even raining."

It was as if Mittens had understood every word Destiny had said because then the beautiful cat walked over to the grand fountain in the middle of the park and leaped in to the crystal blue water.

Destiny jumped up, "I have to save her." and she rushed over to the fountain. When she got to the edge of the water, Mittens was nowhere to be seen. Destiny leaned over the edge of the fountain and peered in further. She saw a gold glow coming from the bottom of the water and suddenly she was sucked into the water and swallowed by the gold glow at the bottom of the fountain. Destiny shut her eyes tight and held her breath until she landed in a soft marshmallow pillow.

When Destiny opened her eyes she looked around and saw people riding on dragons, trees and flowers that were made of delicious sweets which when you pick they grow back right away. There were no cars or litter, everything was so clean. There was a beautiful river of flowing, rich chocolate, wonderful beaches and amazing food.

Mittens ran up to Destiny and they explored this wonderful land together. Destiny ate what her heart desired and played all day long with her furry friend, Mittens.

Just when Destiny thought she was in complete paradise, and far, far away from her cramped flat in London, she turned around and saw something that she never thought she would see.

Chapter 4

Destiny looked shocked as she realised that it was her older brother Henry who had obviously followed her without her knowing.

"What are you doing here Henry?" asked Destiny.

"I also wanted to get out of the flat, Destiny, to have freedom," Henry replied.

"But you were on your iPad when I left so you couldn't have noticed that I had gone, and how did you know where I was?"

"I wasn't really on my iPad – I was just pretending so I was able to follow you at a distance."

Destiny began to think that Henry might be a nicer brother than she thought and that he might want to make up for all the arguments that they have had in the past.

"What is this place?" asked Henry. "We've just fallen into the fountain in the little park round the corner from our flat, and now we're in this amazing paradise world!"

"Well, it's all new to me as well, but my friend Mittens led me here," said Destiny

"Who is Mittens?" replied Henry.

"Would you like me to introduce you to her? She's here somewhere..." Destiny looked around and started to call "Mittens! Where are you?"

But the little cat was nowhere to be seen.

Just then Destiny and Henry heard a rustling in the bushes next to them. And then they heard crying and whining. They got down on their knees and crawled along the bottom of the bushes until they saw a little clearing in the bushes. Tucked away in the twigs and the leaves was Mittens, huddled up into a ball.

"Don't be scared," said Destiny and Mittens

looked up, but looked over at Henry. She started to tremble with fear and she backed away.

Chapter 5

"I think she's scared of you," said Destiny to Henry. "Maybe she knows that you've been mean to me in the past."

Henry looked sad. Suddenly Henry put out his hand and tried to stroke Mittens.

"I'm sorry if I've scared you, you don't need to be frightened of me. Sometimes I can be a bit mean but I don't mean it. Sometimes I feel like I can't say how I feel but I'm a kind person inside."

Just then Mittens walked out of the bushes and came over to Henry and cuddled into him, and started purring. Henry stroked her and smiled.

"And Destiny, you're the best sister and I'm so sorry that I've been mean to you. I just didn't know how to tell you that I love you and I want to be your friend."

Destiny smiled at her brother and the three friends came together for a big hug.

"Thank you Henry, now I understand," said Destiny. "I didn't really think you were a mean person. Now, we should enjoy the paradise world altogether!"

For the rest of the afternoon the friends explored and played in the paradise world. Destiny climbed the trees and ate the jelly fruits. Mittens rolled in the soft grass. And Henry fell into the chocolate river, but it wasn't a problem and he enjoyed swimming and drinking the chocolate. When the others saw him, they jumped in too.

Then, the stars came out in the beautiful sky and Destiny and Henry realised it was time to go home.

"Where does Mittens live?" said Henry.

"She doesn't have a home, I've always just seen her in the park," replied Destiny. "Shall we take her home with us?"

"Yes!" said Henry excitedly. "So whenever we want to come back to our special paradise world, we can. Let's go home!"

"Mittens, would you like to come and live with us?" asked Destiny.

And the little cat meowed and jumped on them,

So the three friends jumped into the fountain, landed back in the park and walked home to their flat to start their new life together.

Cat-astrophy
By Xanthe

All cats can talk but nobody knows how to listen to them. Do you know? Well I do. This is what happened last weekend, to a cat called Dashy. You see, Dash, who lives with very organised people, doesn't find her owners very interesting. In fact she finds them extremely boring. They never play with her, so she spends most of her time outside.

Anyway, one Saturday morning, her owners

decided to have a holiday. There were four people in the family, two big ones and two smaller ones. One of the bigger ones was often called something like 'Dad', and the other big one was called... 'Mum'? The two smaller ones were called Bob and Beth. Mum ordered Bob and Beth around, whilst Dad packed food. Dash sat on the windowsill ordering them about in her own way.

"Annoying humans, they don't listen," thought Dash. So Dash actually couldn't wait until her owners left. It meant she could have a party! Finally her family finished packing and went away in their car (or, as Dash called it, 'Big Loud Monster'.)

"Aha! The house is mine!" miaowed Dash.

For Dash's big party, she needed to ask all her cat mates to come round (with their instruments) to her house, at night of course! So that is exactly what she did, house after house, catflap after catflap. She had to ask fifteen cats – FIFTEEN!!! You can probably see why she was tired!

When the night arrived, so did all the cats. They were loaded with violins, flutes, clarinets, saxophones, trumpets and horns. They also had bags and bags full of mice-cream ingredients. They were going to have so much fun tonight!

Once the cats had finished unpacking their 'borrowed' instruments, they started playing music. Fast and slow, quiet and LOUD. The cats were jumping and dancing around the house, on the table and chairs, on the sofa and TV. When they were all tired out, they made mice-cream and broke into the tins of cat food with their claws. After they were stuffed full, it was about half-past midnight, so they all went home. Dashy picked the comfiest bed and quickly fell asleep.

When Dash woke up, she realised that she had covered the bed with muddy paw-prints.

"Oh no!" miaowed Dash. She thought about what to do. Then she had an idea. Dash started licking the bed until she had made the mud disappear. After she had cleaned up, Dash scampered down the stairs and went to look for some breakfast. However, when she got downstairs she saw that a glass of mice-cream had fallen over – it was CHAOTIC! Dash didn't know what to do, so she took it step by step.

"Well, I know my owners usually come back at 10 o'clock, and it's six now, so that means

97

I have four hours," Dashy reminded herself. That might sound long to you, but for a cat that's like a minute. The mice-cream disaster had caused two messes: a great big puddle of mice-cream oozing across the floor, complete with shards of glass that were scattered in the puddle.

Dash thought about what a person would do (not her owners, because they would be shrieking!). She didn't have an idea though, so she tried to sweep up the glass with her tail, but she was unimpressed about getting very mice-creamy.

After she had finished tidying up the glass, she looked at the clock and... Oh no! She only had two hours left! What was she going to do about the mice-cream? Then an idea popped up into her head, but it was quite a courageous one: she would have to venture into the garage and work out how to use the hoover!

Dash padded over to the kitchen to see how she could open the garage door. She decided to use her tactic for opening the bedroom door, and that was by jumping onto the handle. So that is what she did. Dash climbed onto the wooden chopping board, and from there, she leapt elegantly and landed on the door handle. The door swung open, and a blast of cold air blew at her body, which made her shiver all the way down her spine.

The garage was very big, very dark, but because of Dash's good eyesight, she could see that is was extremely organised. She started to scan the vast room for the hoover. Something glinted in the corner, because light was cutting through the dark like a sharp knife. She followed the beam of light and reached out her paw, and she touched cold, polished plastic.

"Yes!" Dash exclaimed, and she knocked the hoover down with her head. Dash pushed the hoover towards the dim light of the kitchen. When she had got there, Dash pulled the door closed, and tried to work out how to turn it on. She thought it had been magic how her owners had turned it on, so she tried some magic phrases of her own.

"Miaow-bra-CAT-dabra!"

Nothing happened. She tried to think what her humans would say, but she realised that they had said absolutely nothing. She searched for something to help her, but found nothing but a big, black button. She tried pressing it, and a horrible noise came out of the hoover. It made her fur stand up on end!

"Honestly, why did I ever make myself do this?" miaowed Dash over the noise. She ran over to the sofa and buried herself in the cushions for five minutes, until she finally decided to try again. She braced herself against the noise, and took a peek at the clock. "Oh no! I only have an hour and a half left!" Dash exclaimed. "I have to do this." She went back to the hoover, but she ran straight back to the sofa. This happened multiple times before she decided to finally, really do this.

She pushed the vacuum cleaner with her head, telling herself that she bet she would be deaf after this. She sucked up the sloppy mice-cream off the floor, and polished it with her tail.

Dash said to herself, "Five minutes until they come home!" She quickly tidied the sofa cushions and rushed over to a chair and pretended to be asleep.

"Hello, we're back!" announced Mum.

"Dashy!" Bob and Beth squealed as they ran over to give Dash a hug. It was the tightest hug ever: it made her squeal because she had eaten lots last night!

As soon as they went to unpack, Dashy ran outside to meet her friends. A few minutes later, she heard screams coming from the bedroom because the parents had just realised their bed was soaked in cat-lick!

Dash sniggered, and went on another adventure, but I wont tell you that just now. I told you I could speak cat language! Why don't you try to listen to your animal next time?

The Secret Life of Nimbus

By Ailsa

Have you ever wondered why a cat goes missing for a while then comes back like nothing happened? Well, this is the life of a particularly clumsy cat by the name of Nimbus.

Night 1

I was sitting in my favourite place, sunbathing as usual, when I felt my feet leaving the ground. Oh, I definitely realised what was going on, I was flying! I properly realised when I flew through a cloud, I went through the atmosphere too. I had a good look at Mercury and a peep at Saturn but whilst re-entering the atmosphere, I accidentally turned myself into a comet.

Night 2

After the space incident, I decided to go swimming. I dived in, not thinking, and got swept out by a massive wave. I had a good time swimming with the fish and diving with the dolphins until I realised I was far out at sea. Then I found out I was down the Mariana Trench – I wondered why the fish were glowing – and had to get out.

Night 3

This idea did not contain water: I was going to climb Mount Everest, the tallest mountain in the world.

Helmet, yes. Rope, yes. Cat food, 1. Warm things? No. Who needs warm stuff when you've got fur?

RESULTS: getting to the top – I made it!!!

Side effects were: icicles on my tail and my ears were solid blocks of ice.

Luckily, I do know how to make a fire. I thawed out by the next morning. Well how was I to know that it was really cold on Mount Everest? The good news was that the food was absolutely delicious – I got extra treats when I got home and then I found a fish in the bin.

Night 4

I did not think that this would end in a tragedy. How wrong I was! It was in the Amazon Jungle – I was a Ninja swinging on the vines and jumping through the trees making no noise at all (almost). It was hot, wet and moist. There were lots of crocodiles but no cats. Well, there were no cats anywhere else I went. The birds were cool, not like any I've seen before, and there were capybaras and frogs – lots of frogs – and monkeys, chameleons and snakes. I was going along wonderfully, swinging through the trees like a monkey then I fell into a swamp. It was really, really stinky and had piranhas in it. Not going there again.

Night 5

No danger in this one. No risks. I've risk-assessed everything that can go wrong (almost). The one and only best thing in the world where nothing can go wrong is ... the best thing in the world is ... my favourite thing is ... should I have said it by now?
SLEEPING - nothing can go wrong with that.
ZZZZZZ

Cat Gone Missing!

By Imogen

Not so long ago there was a ginger tabby cat, called Kevin, he lived just at the edge of town with Mr Button, Mrs Button and their two children Ellie and Max. Ellie is thirteen, Max is nine and Mr Button and Mrs Button are...well...it would be rude to tell you their age.

Kevin's life was almost perfect until this annoying dog called Rolo (weird name, I know) came along and ruined everything!

For over a month or so Rolo made everything worse. Well it only seemed to affect Kevin's life, because everyone else absolutely loved Rolo.

Rolo was constantly chasing Kevin out of the house and up and down the streets. The only safe place for Kevin was up in an apple tree.

Eventually Kevin got fed up! And decided to LEAVE HOME!

He was going to tell everyone but they were too busy stroking Rolo. So right away he started packing and then began his journey.

He had been walking for a while when it started to get late, which meant that he had to find a place to stop. Sadly, the best Kevin could find was a bin down a creepy, narrow alley. It wasn't quite what he was looking for but I guess you can't expect much from a small hidden away street.

After Kevin got himself 'comfortable' he dozed off for the night.

Early the next morning Kevin woke up... to the sight of three cats! They were Tiger, Storm and Scar. They were staring down at him awfully too close. He was so scared he leapt out of the bin and onto the ground!

"Who are you and what are you doing right there?" exclaimed Kevin,

"I'm Scar and this is Tiger and Storm," the toughest looking cat said in a deep, menacing growl, "and this is our turf."

"There is one rule around here," he went on, "and that one rule is whoever comes in here never comes out!"

Now Kevin was starting to regret running away from home as he thought about sitting on the carpet by the warm, cosy, fireplace. Now that he had met Scar, Rolo didn't seem that bad at all. He spent the rest of that day scavenging in the bin for any tiny morsel of food he could find. Before he knew it, it was dark out, the stars were shining bright and he was feeling sleepy. He settled down in his bin to get some sleep, wishing he was back at home.

"Psst, psst, are you awake?" Storm whispered. "Well I am now," said Kevin in a tired voice, "What do you want?"

"I want to get you out of here," she replied

"But why are you helping me, I thought you didn't like me?" he questioned.

"I'm not one of them," Storm said, "I got stuck here just like you and I had to join their gang because that was the only way to get food and water. But it's not too late for you. We can get you out tonight, while they are asleep. I know a way to sneak out the back.

There is a gap in the fence. It is too small for Scar and Tiger to get through, but we can."

"Ok, I agree, it will be risky but it is better than staying here," Kevin said. "But I don't know the way home from the back, can you show me?"

"Yes, but I'll have to be back by morning," agreed Storm.

So they quietly tiptoed to the back of the alley. Luckily cats can be very quiet at times like this. They went behind one of the many bins and saw the hole in the fence. They ducked down and made themselves as small as they could. Storm went through first, but as Kevin was a house cat he wasn't as skinny as Storm so he got a bit stuck. While he was struggling he knocked a bin over which made a loud clatter! Suddenly Tiger woke up, Kevin froze as still as he could, while Tiger was looking around to see what had made the noise. Luckily Storm had quick thinking and pulled Kevin through the fence in time.

Off they ran, as happy and jolly as a dog with a ball! Free from the alleyway and Scar and Tiger's trap. Storm led him through the streets until they reached Kevin's house.

"Here you are, this is your chance to be free,"

said Storm. "Thank you, thank you, thank you," said Kevin, "I should have realised I'm definitely not a street cat before I ran away, I would hate living out here."

"Yes it is extremely hard," whimpered Storm.

"Well then why don't you come in and live with me? My family would take you in, they love all animals" said Kevin.

Storm looked at him as if she was about to cry, and suddenly burst out, "Thank you, thank you, thank you, this is the kindest thing anyone has ever done for me."

Together they went through Kevin's catflap. His family were still fast asleep, so they waited by the fireplace, chatting and laughing until the morning when Storm would meet her new family.

The Brown Mysterious Box

By Iqra

On one sunny morning, at the front of Evan's family's doorstep was a box. Not a particular box but a mysterious, brown and noisy box.

When they hear a knock they walk slowly to the door and Mr Evan says "I wonder who could that be" and he opens the door and finds an unexpected box.

They are all confused and a bit scared when they hear a rattling sound. They bring the box in and open it and find a black and white striped cat.

Mr Evan takes the cat out and spots a note, they open the note and it says *'Give this cat a new home, love and care'.*

Emily who is a member of the family comes home from school She is quite shy to come near the cat but tries to touch its furry fur. Emily strokes the cat gently and smiles. Emily notices the cat has a golden collar with blue stripes and has the number 917.

The cat and Emily become friends and Emily's dad tells her all about the brown box outside their doorstep and what the letter said. Emily continues to look after the cat and names her Tabby.

Later that day Emily and Tabby had fun and played games, they played hide and seek, catch me, fetch it and Emily liked the catch me game because it was active.

Emily thinks Tabby also liked the catch me game.

Emily used all her pocket money to buy Tabby's new toys. In the weekend Emily took her cat for a walk and popped to her friend Sara's house who also has a cat. Her cat is called Libby. Libby and Tabby played together and had great fun.

After the school holidays Emily and her dad

walked to school. As Emily was walking she saw a cat poster on a wall.

She asked her dad "Dad, what is that?"

"What is what?" Replied Mr Evan.

"That poster on the wall," said Emily.

"It is a missing cat poster. It means if you see this cat then you need to call the owner on the number given and the owner will claim that cat."

"Ah ok" says Emily, as she walks into the school building.

Emily had a great time at school and shared her experience with her new cat found in a mystery brown box. At the end of the day Emily was waiting for her dad to pick her up. While she is waiting she walks closer to the missing cat poster and finds out the cat on the poster is Tabby.

At the moment Emily is in shock and starts crying. Her dad asks Emily "What is the matter?"

Emily replies, "It's the cat poster we saw earlier and it's Tabby because it looks like Tabby and it has the same golden collar with blue stripes and the number is 917."

Emily's dad takes a photo of the poster and they go home and tell Mrs Evan all about it.

That evening Mr and Mrs Evan tried to comfort Emily to be happy because she did the right thing by noticing the cat was Tabby and being honest leads to happiness.

The next day they ring the owner and say they have the cat and invite him over. When the owner sees Tabby he is so happy and runs over to see Tabby. However, Tabby takes a step back and runs back to Emily and pounces on her lap. Emily walks to the owner with Tabby and as they get closer and closer Tabby starts to recognise the owner. Emily kneels down and the owner is happy to get his cat back.

The owner walks out through the door and Emily starts crying and the owner hears Emily.

The owner tells Emily, "Emily you can keep the cat because you have a kind heart and a loving heart".

"Thank you so much" says Mr Evan.

"Thank you," Emily says with a smile.

Emily's dad asked "Who left the note and the box with Tabby?" The owner said he was very sick and wasn't well enough to look after the cat so his busy and old wife gave the cat away.

When the owner got better he started

searching for his cat. "If the cat wants to visit me, my door number is 917."

Emily noticed "That number is on Tabby's collar" The owner doesn't live too far from the Evan family. Emily is very happy to keep Tabby forever.

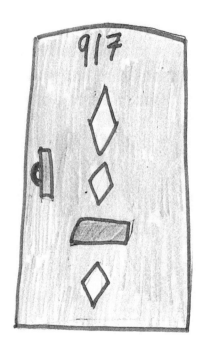

The Catastrophe

By Lana

Chapter 1 – THE MISSING MAYOR

Once upon a time in a far-off place called Kitty City, in a tall building in the town square there lived a cat called Archie. His lovely mother cat Thea, lives with him and she loves to bake delicious snacks for him.

Archie is a fluffy soft ginger cat and is also a famous detective. Archie has been called a lot recently by different police officers, because Roger, the mean black cat, has been very suspicious and is up to his old tricks.

"Mum, I know what Roger's doing to be suspicious. It all adds up, because..." Archie explained.

"Kiddo, go to bed," interrupted Mum.

"But Mum! I need to tell you how it all adds up!"

"Ok, go on."

"So, Roger doesn't like parties, but he asked to come to Lulu's 50th birthday party. You know, Lulu the Town Mayor Tabby cat. When he got there, he was holding a HUGE present for Lulu, He went into the corner of the room and unwrapped the present himself. It was a cage! He asked to dance with Lulu and during the dance, he went into the corner of the room where the cage was and chucked her in it!!" shouted Archie. "And he said to Lulu 'this is your present hahohaa'. Lulu the mayor was very, and I mean very, upset."

"Ooookk... now to bed," said his mum.

"Aaaah" he said in a sad voice. "Anyway, I'm not a kid anymore, but fine, I'll go to bed on one condition," said Archie.

"Ok. What's the condition?" replied his Mum.

"That you'll let me tell you something."

"Mmm, go ahead."

"Tomorrow," said Archie, "I'm going away for a few days, and I mean, it's already prepared because I'm in charge of finding out why Roger's being suspicious, why he's taken Lulu and I will find her and bring her home. Because everyone is going crazy without her."

"No kiddo! Don't go!" exclaimed Mum.

"Mum, my name is Archie, you know because you named me. I'm not a kid anymore! I'm 32."

"Fine, Archie, please don't go."

"Sorry mum I have to go and I don't want to

upset my friends and I don't want to lose my job. So yeah, about that, and by the way it is already booked."

"NO, you're not going! It's not safe!"

"No, no mum please I want to go."

"If you want to go then you're going with me."

"NO, you are not going with me, OK?!" Shouted Archie.

Archie had a plan. He would tell his mum to meet him at the airport at 11am but he would go at 9am in the morning by himself.

Chapter 2 – THE MYSTERIOUS FIGURE

So, the next morning, Archie left at 9am. He felt a bit mean because he tricked his mum, but it had to be done. He landed after 4 annoying hours, because he was sitting next to a crying tabby cat who was a baby. And it wouldn't stop crying! Anyway, on with the story.

Archie grabbed his suitcase and went off. He took his magnifying glass out of his suitcase and looked for paw prints,

"Yes!" shouted Archie. He put his paw pad in the mud and covered it and licked it.

"Fresh!" he said. He lifted his head and

followed the paw prints. Suddenly he saw a shadow in the distance. He ran after it. He ran and ran and ran, with no idea where he was going. Then he lost sight of the mysterious shadow, but he kept going through the path.

He came across a thistle bush and saw a bit of colour on it, he went over to it and saw that the colour was cat fur. He took it off and put it in his pocket in case it was important.

He kept searching and searching and searching, until he came across the trail of paw prints that he saw earlier, so he continued to follow them. The pawprints stopped at a big rock. Archie lifted the rock up and there, he saw.... can you guess what it was?!

It was the cage with Lulu the Mayor in it!

Archie jumped down and got his big chunky bolt cutters from his suitcase and chopped the lock. Clink, clunk, clink! The cage door swung open. Lulu climbed out and thanked Archie.

"Thank you so much for saving me!" she exclaimed.

They used their cat skills to climb out of the hole under the stone. They saw the shadow again, so they started running towards it, to find out who it was. They kept running and running and running. After an hour of following the figure, they stopped for breath and to glug down some water from Archie's suitcase. While they stopped, they realised they needed a plan, So, they started thinking about how to catch the figure that trapped Lulu.

Chapter 3 – THE PLAN

Archie realised that he had a piece of rope in his bag. They could tie it into a lasso to capture the figure, but they'd have to be very cunning and get close enough to reach htm. After a few minutes of trying to make the lasso, they managed to do it. They crept up behind a bush and then they waited for the figure to return. They waited for 10 minutes and suddenly the figure came back and Archie threw the lasso into the air and swung it round and caught the figure.

"We got him! it's Roger!" shouted Archie.
"Yes!" Lulu cried.

Chapter 4 – THE QUESTIONS

They took Roger to where Archie was staying, and they questioned him for a while.

"Roger, give me the answers to my questions. Why have you been suspicious recently?

Why did you hide Mayor Lulu? She hasn't been happy about it. Why did you run from us when you knew you'd done something bad?"

"Sorry, I just wanted to be mayor. I am so sorry," Roger said in a feeble voice. Then Archie understood that Roger wasn't trying to be mean.

So, Archie forgave him. Archie had finished the mission, so they went home the next day. Archie and Roger went to the city hall and Roger stood on the platform and apologised. And there were lots of claps and applause and cheers. Then cats of all sizes and shapes hugged Roger.

"Aaah! That's too many hugs!" Roger shouted and he ran home, and everyone laughed.

Mayor Lulu was safe and sound, quickly got back to running the town and was relieved that Archie had saved her. Roger never disturbed her again and everyone lived happily ever after.

The Hole in the Fence
By Lauren

One sunny day Jimmy and Rose were playing in the garden. Jimmy was a yellow and brown stripy cat. Rose was a black cat with a long, white tail which was soft and fluffy. They were good friends who loved to chase each other and climb on things. Rose lived in a round, cosy cottage with a pointed roof and Jimmy lived next door. Every day they went through a hole in the fence to play together. Today they were in Jimmy's garden which was very long with lots of trees and colourful flowers. Rose was running after Jimmy trying to catch him, but he was going very fast, as fast as a leopard.

Suddenly, Jimmy ran up one of the trees. This tree was really big with lots of leaves and the bark was soft and old. Rose stopped because she couldn't climb up that tree. It was too high for her. "Come down," shouted Rose. Jimmy looked down and thought how high it was.

He felt scared. "I'm stuck and scared. I can't get down," he cried. "Can you help me?" he asked.

"I can't get up that tree to help you," she said worriedly. "What should I do?" she thought to herself...

Excitedly, she had an idea. She ran off as quickly as she could to get her owners. She ran back through the hole in the fence to her own garden. She pounced at the back door and landed like a starfish. Her owner heard a big crash and came to the door. She was an eight year old girl called Lily.

"What's the matter, silly cat?" she giggled. Rose meowed loudly and ran back down the garden. Lily followed her to see what was the matter. She looked over the wooden fence and saw Jimmy in the tree.

"Oh no, he must be stuck," she exclaimed. Lily raced back to her cottage and called out for her older sister, Lola, who was fifteen years old. Lily explained what happened to

Jimmy and Lola went to get the neighbour who found a ladder. They went to the tree and Jimmy's owner climbed up the ladder and rescued Jimmy. She gave him a big hug and he meowed

"Thank you for saving me," to Rose.

Jimmy's owner said "Don't go up that tree again!"

The Story of the First Cat

by Barnabus

The Stone Age

My tale begins perhaps dead at the edge of dusk. I woke up just to see a dry deserted harsh wasteland. As the years went by, I honed my abilities to kill humans, otherwise known as cavemen. Knowing these cavemen also possessed power over me, it could potentially be either a good idea or a bad idea to attack them. I had never seen any of my bloodthirsty kind, all I saw was fight after fight and death after death and victory after victory.

The Bronze Age

As the humans became smarter making bronze, I hid in the shadows of my past and what I had witnessed. I also began to become less fierce. My friends withered away until I was the only one left. Food was scarce and I was lucky to find a supply of it. But this night could have been my last! I woke up in the middle of the night in a small, lonely cage. Five humans came to see me.

One of them said "We should do tests on the tiger". As they chatted more and more, my rage grew like fearsome fire. I pounced at my cage, knocking it off the huge pit. The door of the cage opened and I sprang out ready to pounce. I jumped on them and ate their flesh ravenously. The last human escaped. Then a flaming arrow came down and hit the cage I had been in. The whole room was set on fire and the remains of flesh burned hot and steaming.

The Iron Age

It all went dark. I woke to see two beings. One called Stirbro the god of past ages wearing a long stretched white cloak, fur skins stained with blood and a white shimmering chain mail helmet. The second, Therdafer, the god of decisions of life. He was wearing skulls from both animals and humans who had passed their life to him. After a long disagreement Therdafer won the argument to keep me alive to make something new. All of a sudden I was falling through the ocean blue sky, panting in fear of death. Then I closed my eyes and found myself in my damp cave. But there was something else, shining in the dark with orange sun fur. She was like me, a memory forgotten by the gods themselves. We slowly bonded over the years and soon our first children arrived. Not like us, we called them cats. A new age was upon us, the age of cats. It was time for sabre toothed tigers to go and cats to thrive.

Action Cat – In Space!
By Andrew

Once in Hollywood there was a cat stuntman who performed the most amazing stunts the world had ever seen. His most famous stunts included flying low in a helicopter over an erupting VOLCANO, riding a rickety rowing boat over a waterfall to the Great Wall of China, and motorbiking over a shark-infested lake! He loved doing all these exciting stunts, but always looked for his next adventure. Then he heard about a movie, not any old movie, the BEST-MOVIE-OF-ALL-TIME!!!!

It was an action movie, set in outer space. In it, the main character gets blasted off into space where he meets some aliens. Some aliens were nice, but there were others who were trying to destroy Earth. In the movie, their mission was to protect the planet and defeat the invasion.

It sounded like the adventure he was waiting for, and he rushed to audition. He had to show his motorbike skills, bravery, and expert fighting skills. Later that day he received a phone call – he'd got the job!

Once he had signed-up for the movie, the first thing they did was to put him into a cannon and fired him high into the air. The safety net was supposed to stop him flying into space, he was meant to hit the net then fall down into a swimming pool and to swim to safety. But something had happened to the net and instead of splashing in the water, Action Cat crashed through the roof of the studio and was blasted into space!!!!

Luckily, he was wearing a real NASA spacesuit which protected him. He zoomed past the moon, space station and planets.

Action Cat was nearly out of air when a green beam of light pulled him up into a spaceship!

Inside the spaceship a strange, muffled voice asked him if he was okay "Okay, are you?"

Action Cat answered "I would be better, but I did just almost DIE in space. But thanks."

He wondered who it was asking the question. When he looked up, he saw aliens! He tried to run away, he feared they were going to eat him. He cried out "AAAALLIEEEEENS!!!!!! I don't even taste nice."

Action cat looked closer at the aliens; There were lots of them. They all looked different, except two who he thought might be twins. One looked like a person, one floated like a balloon, and another looked very much like a dog. One even had at least 10 tentacles, an upside-down mouth above his single eye and wriggled around the room.

"Easy, woah!" The floating alien said, "Us Aliens help you nice."

Action Cat wasn't sure at first, but stopped running away and thought they seemed friendly. The aliens started playing some alien hip-hop music, which he tried to dance along to, but didn't want to try their food. The food looked like eyeballs in jelly and cake with slime icing.

After everyone had gone to bed, Action Cat was still wide awake. He went to explore the spaceship and found the kitchen. He was eating some cookies when he heard some aliens enter the room. They were talking quietly, and he crept over to listen. The alien leader, called Boss was discussing his plans to completely destroy the earth to make room for a giant alien cake-ship! He had set-up some lasers, and once they got close enough to Earth, he just needed to press the fire button. He told the other aliens in the room they were only 5 minutes away.

Action Cat ran to find the friendly aliens and cried "Help! Your boss is trying to destroy my planet! Please don't let him press the button!!"

Action Cat and 9 friendly aliens all rushed through into the control room. Boss and his alien friends were already there.

"Please don't press the button," said Action Cat.

"Why?" said Boss.

Action cat replied, "We're friendly and haven't hurt you." Boss laughed and floated towards the button. There was a fight and Action Cat bit him, but while the fight goes on *BOSS HITS THE FIRE BUTTON.*

Action cat searches the room for something, anything, to escape the spaceship and to stop the laser from hitting Earth. He spots a space bike in the corner of the control room. Action Cat jumps on while the other friendly aliens open a hatch and help fight away Boss and his evil alien friends. Once the latch is open, he zooms out on the space bike!!!!!!!

Luckily, he was an amazing motorbike stuntman. It reminded him of when he had to jump over the shark-infested lake. He rode towards the laser beam. Just before he rode into it, he pressed the ejector button. He only just survived by an inch!!!!! He landed on a satellite, but he was too heavy for it and it began to fall to Earth.

Action Cat thought this was the end... he fell and fell... right into the studio swimming pool. The film crew clapped and cheered; they thought it was all part of his stunt. They asked him why it had taken him so long, and he explained the whole story. They didn't believe it until the friendly aliens, having defeated Boss and his evil friends came down to Earth in their spaceship.

Action Cat became famous throughout the Earth and the universe!!!!!!!!!!

The Dog Who Liked the Cat

by Maya

In the peaceful town of Fiddleberry, there was a beautiful young woman who lived in a small cottage with her extraordinary pet called Max. Max was a kind-hearted dog who loved everyone, including most animals. However, there was one specific animal he absolutely dreaded! CATS!!! Most dogs didn't like cats but he really hated cats.

One day, his owner had just arrived from work, and as she walked through the door she held his greatest enemy, a CAT!!! Max was absolutely furious about this. He definitely knew he had to live with it. He couldn't help but charge at his owner around the room until she locked him in, as punishment. As the days passed, Max kept his distance from the cat. He found out her name was Lily, and found it sort of interesting. He was suddenly starting to like cats.

The next morning, Max finally decided that he would talk to Lily. He had never talked to a cat so he was very nervous. He crept over to the door and peered through a gap to see what Lily was doing. She was rather quiet, but it looked like she was playing with a stripy pink ball hanging from a thin yellow string. Max watched her for hours on end while gazing in amazement at her silky coat of white fur and her gleaming blue and green eyes, After a quiet moment of thinking, Max sneakily tiptoed into the room.

As he walked towards her, Lily took no notice of of him as she still thought Max didn't like her.

"Look Lily, let me explain," sighed Max. Lily silently looked up at him to see what explanation he had to say. As he spoke and spoke, she noticed he looked more friendly than she'd ever expected.

When Max had finished he apologised and said, "I'm sorry, I shouldn't have tried to attack you when I should've greeted you. It's just that I was forced by my family to hate cats."

"Well, I'm sorry too. I should've spoken to you sooner," whispered Lily.

"It's okay," replied Max. "We all make mistakes." They happily shook paws and started playing with the stripy pink ball Lily was using earlier. After quite a long time of playing, they finally settled down and fell asleep on the sofa.

The next morning Max and Lily watched their owner leave the house for work and they went to eat the breakfast that she had given them. They both ate slowly thinking of what to do for the rest of the day.

"I think that we should sneak out the house!" exclaimed Lily.

"That's a great idea!" replied Max.

They both agreed, then finished their meal and jumped up on a shelf to climb out of the open window Lily saw earlier. There was only one floor so the jump would be easy. Lily went first and helped Max get down too for he had never in his life jumped from a window. They made sure the coast was clear and quickly scurried off into the dense woods. As they trotted through the path, towering trees hung over them, filling up the bright blue sky. There were fluttering birds flying over colourful shades of green leaves, desperately trying to get towards their nest of sweet chicks, who were waiting for a delicious meal. There was fresh soil, with endless rows of delicate flowers covering its damp, earthy brown look, while sweet yellow bees buzzed all over the place choosing which flower to collect juicy pollen from.

After many hours of walking, there was a rustle in the bushes nearby.

"What on earth was that?" Max whispered.

"I don't know but it doesn't sound good." Replied Lily. As they listened, the sound inched closer and closer and closer! Until out of nowhere a nasty looking pit bull emerged out of the bushes and stomped towards them. He had an enormous body, large floppy ears and red beady eyes like fire. He had scars all over him and thick, oozy dribble slowly dripping out from his large muzzle.

"Hello Lily," said the stranger in a hoarse but evil voice.

"How does he know your name?" Questioned Max in confusion.

"He ate my mother," whispered Lily in anger, her eyes filling with tears. She stared at the stranger in disgust as he stood there in triumph.

"Your mother was weak. I was very hungry, so she was my only option. Besides, she was quite tasty." He said.

"You will pay for this!" cried Lily. At once she

pounced onto his dirty back and scratched him several times with her sharp pointy claws while biting at him furiously. He threw her off and she flew into the colossal oak tree. Max howled in frustration and hastily charged at him then bit him tightly around the leg before being thrown to the ground. Both were very injured but kept on going to defeat him. Max threw a few more scratches and dodged his death-dealing bite. At last they did one more tackle and he finally retreated. They knew that he would never come back again.

Dirty and scarred, Max limped over to a pond nearby and had a cool, soothing bath to help soothe his pain. Lily licked her fur to make sure everything was squeaky clean and washed. They both checked if anyone was there and finally set off back home. They raced out of the forest, past the streets and carefully jumped back through the cottage window before their owner arrived from work.

Amazingly, when she opened the door, she didn't notice anything out of the usual.

A Day in the Life of a Tiger

By Aimee

I am known for my elegance and I am a smokey grey tabby cat. My belly is as white as snow, but my stripes are as dark as the night. Some may say I'm a bit on the chunkier side, but I think I'm the cutest thing since.... I don't even know! I am going to take you through a day of my busy life....

In the morning, you can find me snoozing on my cat tree. I love my cat tree, it's grey like me, and as soft as my silky fur. I will be sleeping in a little round pod, all curled up so I stay nice, warm and cosy. I silently wait here, for my servants to come and feed me. I can smell chicken today. Mmmm I love chicken... My favourite food is tuna.. But I just love food, so I can't complain!

My servant brings me a delicious plate of chicken flakes. I wait for them to pick me up and place me beside my food, and then I take a few little licks to see if it tastes as good as it smells. I think I've started to drool a little! This is taster than I thought it could ever be.. Soon I start to devour it... Mmmmmmm, it feels like heaven in my mouth.

Now that I've finished eating my breakfast, my tummy feels very full so I go back to have a little snooze in the round pod on my cat tree. My favourite servant, the little one, comes to give me kisses and tells me that she loves me... And then they disappear.

I gaze out of the window, watching the birds fly in the sky, thinking that one day, I may be able to catch one.. Oh how it may taste... Probably much tastier than this chicken... I see the leaves blowing in the wind. They've blown off the trees now, making them seem very bare. Wait, what is that noise? Oh no! My brothers are awake and have come to annoy me... I'm not too keen on them yet. I like to whack them on the head when they come too close.

I jump down off my cat tree and have another look through the patio doors. It looks so windy outside, I think I'll go for a morning stroll. I strut down the stairs, through the hallway and lounge as if I own the place. Who am I kidding? I am the master of this household! I take a quick peek through my little door and exit my home through it.

The wind feels so good in my fur. I can feel it going through me, sending a few shivers down my spine. My whiskers are tickling me. I quickly jump up the fence and this is the hard part... Walking along the top of the fence. They haven't bothered to paint it, it's still just a boring old beige colour. All of the gardens here are so close together which means I have to walk across the top of the fences to get to the field, I find this quite difficult but I think I've finally managed to master it! I've always been a quick learner.

I have to be careful crossing the road to get to the field, there are really big giant things that keep trying to run me over!

Finally, I've made it safely to the field. Wait what is that? It's one of those delicious looking birds. My belly starts to rumble. I hide in the long green grass, ready to pounce. The bird, who is big, plump and juicy is on top of a rock. It looks so scrumptious. When I am ready to pounce, I always wiggle my big bottom, here I go.... Wiggle, wiggle, wiggle.

Pounce! I land on the fire orange bird, it's feathers start to fall onto the grass. I quickly run back over the road, jump on top of the fence and dart through my little door back into my home. I shall show my servants that I've brought  them a special gift. I hope they appreciate it. I would love to just scoff this bird down right now.

Suddenly, my servants come home and find the bird, I am excited to show them and start meowing around their legs. They keep muttering something, I'm not sure what they are saying but guess what! They chuck the bird outside!!! That delicious dinner has gone to waste!! All the effort I put into that, oh dear. Time to go back onto my cat tree, I'm tired now. That's enough excitement for one day.

The Best Day Ever: The Other Side of the Tracks

By Jessica

A long time ago in a place called Woodchester lived a white spotty cat with brown eyes, and his name was Noah. Noah lived in a smelly junkyard next to the railway track. He was very fed up because he had been stuck in this junkyard all alone since his owner died 5 years ago. On the other side of the railway track was a dark gloomy alley where a ginger cat with blue eyes lived. His name was Jack. Jack also lived alone with no family or any nice cosy place to live in.

Noah often spent the day watching the trains zoom past. One sunny day Noah decided he would take the risk of crossing the railway line to see what was actually on the other side. Without looking he slowly started to cross the track, not realising a train was heading straight for him.

Before he had a chance to realise what was going to happen, a ginger cat appeared out of the darkness of the alley and pounced on Noah to push him clear of the track, as the train passed by.

The ginger cat introduced himself: "Hello, my name is Jack, what's your name?"

"Noah," he muttered.

"Why were you trying to cross that dangerous track?" Jack asked.

"I need to get out of this smelly junkyard. I've been here far too long. I don't have any family or home to go to," Noah replied.

"Neither do I. Let's find a home together," said Jack.

The two cats made a plan to leave the smelly junkyard, navigate their way safely across the railway track and through Jack's dark gloomy alley to a very busy road filled with cars and lorries, driving backwards and forwards. The paths were full of people walking by.

The cats slowly edged out onto the path and into the crowds, but weirdly nobody stopped to look at them or even notice they were there. They felt invisible! They had to come up with another plan to get somebody's attention.

Jack had an idea. He had remembered an empty cardboard box that was left outside the back gate of one of the houses in front of the alley. And so the cats carefully pushed the box out of the alleyway and into the street and put it next to a rubbish bin.

They climbed inside and waited patiently for what seemed like forever when all of a sudden a short old man with a grey beard picked up the box and carried them all the way along the street to a small tidy cottage where he lived.

Once inside the cottage, the cats jumped out of the box and lay down snugly in front of the warm fire.

"Don't worry! I will look after you now," whispered the old man.

From that moment Noah and Jack became best friends and lived a happy and amazing life, and never had to worry again.

Shadow

By Audrey

Most stories start with 'Once upon a time', not this one. This story will start with 'Once upon a shadow'. So, once upon a shadow, there was a young girl (no older than four) rolling around on her carpet. Allie was her name, and she didn't know it yet but she would grow up to be very different to everyone else.

As Allie grew up, people started to notice she was very different to anyone born before. Alie's shadow had a life of its own! It did things Allie hadn't even done that day, such as waved at passers by, even when Allie hadn't lifted up her arm. It had a personality of it's own, cartwheeling around the place even when Allie was standing completely still. The strangest of all, her shadow was there all year round. Even when the sun wasn't out! Her shadow never spoke, but was always there as her silent companion.

We now meet at twelve years old...

Sadly, Allie's shadow is her only friend, since most kids find it a little bit odd. But she's not lonely, Allie likes it that way and life is good. She lives with her mum, dad and brother Tom (who's younger than her by two years)... And they all love Allie's shadow. Well, all of them apart from her cat, Tibbles. Tibbles is one of those cats that no matter how happy they are, their mouth is still in a frown. He is a really fluffy domestic cat, ginger with white stripes. He's always on the hunt for something to bring attention to him, often knocking over flower vases and picture frames.

One morning, when Tibbles was particularly annoyed with Allie's shadow – because the shadow accidentally scared him – he began to hatch a plan. Soon after, Allie and her family found out what that plan was, when Allie made a high pitched scream from upstairs,

"My shadow's gone!" she exclaimed when her family arrived in her room. "Don't worry your father and I will go look for it," suggested mum, trying to reassure Allie, gesturing to her dad to leave.

"I know what you can do," whispered Tom once their parents had left the room. "There's a rumour that in the alley, just down the end our road, is a black cat, but he doesn't have a name so everyone just calls him 'The Oracle'!" he said mysteriously.

"So the cat talks?" asked Allie.

"You know it!" answered Tom and he ran out the room.

Allie felt she had no choice but to believe him. One, because what else could she do? Two, because she knew her brother knew a lot about this sort of thing.

So, that night, under the cover of darkness, Allie crept outside and went down the road in search of 'The Oracle'. Finally she got to the alley, and she had a creepy feeling about the place. Suddenly, there was a scratch, then a clatter of bins. And then silence. Allie had the feeling she was being watched. She turned around, and there, sitting calmly in front of her, was a black cat! A clap of thunder struck.

It started to rain. Allie shivered. "Um, excuse me but... and I know this might sound crazy... but my cat stole my shadow and my brother said you might be able to help me?"

"It it's your shadow you seek,
You'll find it in the place that reeks,
To reunite you with your shadow,
To fix, your sorrow, it's a simple touch,
Let's just hope your cat doesn't mind too much."

That was the riddle of The Oracle

"Okay thanks," replied Allie dashing off to the only place she knew that reeked, the dump behind the supermarket!

Sure enough, when she got there, sitting on the bin was Tibbles, with her shadow in his mouth!

What could she do? Tibbles started hissing, he knew what was coming. All Allie had to do was touch her shadow and all would be okay (according to The Oracle').

She jumped, tried to grasp it, but missed and all in one blur Tibbles got away, Allie tore after him. She cornered him in between two houses and ... and... SHE GOT HER SHADOW BACK!!!! She ran all the way home!

Shockingly, Tibbles was back home the next

day, acting as if nothing had happened, but luckily he never bothered with Allies' shadow again. No one knows quite why!

The next day at school, two girls ran up to Allie and told her they thought her shadow was really cool, they asked if she wanted to play a game. Allie smiled and said yes, maybe she would have a few more friends after all.

The Moon Mammoth
By Daniel

In the NASA headquarters, a small black cat called Bluebell was wandering around everywhere, looking for his owner. With a sudden urge for food, Bluebell walked through a large door, and ended up in a rocket. Like all cats, Bluebell started looking for a space to sleep, and slept on a shelf. He dreamed of flying up to the moon and eating some of it.

Hours later, when he woke up, he noticed an empty glass on the shelf. His instincts kicked in, and he batted the glass off the shelf, and it fell onto the launch button. There was a rumble and the rocket launched with Blubell inside!

Feeling terrified, Bluebell looked out of the window, as Earth got smaller. Suddenly, a crackly voice said: "If you look to your left, you will now see the constellation of the Big Dipper."

"Mmmm, I wonder if it's a chicken dipper?" thought Bluebell.

"To your right, you can see Orion's Belt, off in the distance," the crackly voice blurted from the speaker.

"Hmmm, I wonder if the belt will fit me," pondered Bluebell.

"Straight in front of us is the Milky Way," crackled the mysterious voice.

"Ohhhh, delicious milk," Bluebell purred. "I wonder if there'll be enough for me? Maybe this space thing isn't so bad!"

With surprise, Bluebell noticed he was no longer touching the shelf. He was floating around the cabin like a furry aeroplane. Feeling nervous, he tried to lick his bum, but started rapidly spinning.

Floating past the chair, he dug his claws in, and did a full somersault onto the controls.

Catching Bluebell off guard, the crackly voice announced: "Course changed, now heading to the moon. We will arrive in ten, nine, eight..."

"Argh, I don't want to go to the moon," Bluebell shouted, digging his claws into everything he saw.

"Seven, six, five..."

"I can see the moon coming at me," meowed Bluebell, closing his eyes and going into a cat brace position.

"Four, three, two, one..."

"I'm ready," Bluebell screeched, as they hit the moon like a furry comet.

Quite stunned and dazed, Bluebell saw a hairy snake-like tube coming through the window, and picking him up. When he emerged from the wreckage, he saw it wasn't actually a snake, it was a massive mammoth!

The Moon Mammoth!

Not believing his eyes, Bluebell yowled: "Argh, a mammoth! On the moon! Please don't squish me to a pancake!"

"I'm sorry, I didn't mean to scare you!" bellowed the Moon Mammoth. "I'm Jeff, by the way. What's your name?"

"It's Bluebell," Bluebell squeaked in a small voice. "Are you cross that I'm here?"

"No, I'm so happy that you're here. It's been so lonely on the moon, since I came. A long, long time ago, I was on Earth, and then one night there was a meteor shower. I was sitting on my tree and one of the meteors hit the other end of the tree, and I went flying onto the moon. And I've been here ever since, all on my own," echoed Jeff. "Do you want to play with me? It's been so boring on my own, not being able to play with anyone."

"Of course, I was starting to get bored on

the spaceship," meowed Bluebell.

So Jeff and Bluebell played moon rock stack, where you have to stack as many moon rocks on top of each other before they fall over. And as Bluebell found out, if they fall over, they just go flying all over the moon, never to be seen again. Jeff and Bluebell also gave each other piggybacks. It was quite easy for Jeff, running all around the craters of the moon, with Bluebell hanging on his back for dear life. Bluebell was terrified to put Jeff on his back, but when he got on, Bluebell found out that Jeff weighed nothing, like everything on the moon.

Happy but tired after their fun, Jeff and Bluebell floated back to the wreckage of the spaceship.

"Oh dear," Bluebell howled. "If only my rocket was in one piece, I could get back to Earth to see my family."

"I could help you," trumpeted Jeff. "I'm pretty good at fixing things."

"Of course I want your help fixing this," Blubell purred. "Do you think I could do this all on my own."

It took them what would have been two whole days on Earth to complete the rocket, so that it was able to fly again.

"So, I guess this is goodbye," whimpered Bluebell, as he padded up the stairs to the door. "I'm really going to miss you."

"I'm really going to miss you too," bellowed Jeff as Bluebell shut the door.

Once again, there was a great rumbling sound, as Bluebell's rocket launched back into space. As the rocket drew further and further away, Bluebell saw the silhouette of Jeff, waving his trunk sadly, all alone. But then, Bluebell got an idea. He started batting the controls with his paw.

Back on the moon, Jeff was walking miserably back to his cave, when he heard a great noise. He turned around, and saw Bluebell's rocket screeching to a halt right in front of him.

"What did you forget?" trumpeted Jeff, as Bluebell's head popped out.

"You!" cried Bluebell. "Did you really think I was going to leave you all alone on the moon, with no one else?"

Bluebell leapt onto Jeff's hairy back, and they galloped into his cave, and lived moonily ever after.

Mouse

By Sophie

Just across the road, a few houses down from where I live, there's a cat. It's a beautiful, young, pearl white and charcoal black cat, with a gingery lightning shape on his back. His name is Cinder. Cinder loves to catch mice and leave them on his owners' pillows when they go out. They never enjoy coming home, exhausted, to find a dead mouse. The family Cinder lives with keep him well fed and looked after, as well as giving him plenty of space to play and lots of cuddles. However, one day, Cinder didn't come home...

The family Cinder lives with were frantic, searching everywhere, putting up posters, anything they could think of really. Cinder, however, was loving the freedom and power he had bestowed upon himself. He could do whatever he wanted, whenever he wanted: but the truth is, Cinder really missed his home, all the cuddles – and when he went to sleep at night, all he could think about was the baby, no-one to keep him warm at night, nobody to keep him happy while the family slept soundlessly through the night.

Two weeks later Cinder was starting to get bored of mice and pigeon, maybe even the occasional blackbird – he started to crave beef chunks in jelly. He didn't feel like sleeping in the cold and wet, doing the same things every day. He just wanted to go back to his home. So, Cinder set off the very next day on his journey back to his family and home territory; he travelled all through the day, and finally, as the sun began to set, tinting the sky orange and the clouds pink, he arrived back home. He wandered about on the front step, mewing loudly to attract someone's attention. One of the children, Amy, opened the front door and cried out in sheer joy at seeing her cat again. Neighbours all around stuck their heads out of windows to see what was going on.

Cinder found it exceedingly difficult to settle back into the life of a pet cat. He no longer needed to catch his own food to survive, or make his own places to sleep – often you could find him pacing, lying down in one spot, then getting up and moving somewhere else, only to move on again. His owners kept him inside the house for a few days, then gradually started letting him out again, to avoid any more disappearances.

Cinder loves the outdoors, hates to be confined. He absolutely loved it when he was allowed out at will once again.

One day, as Cinder was walking slowly and gently along the pavement, he smelled his favourite cat treats coming from inside a house he had never seen before. Being a curious and adventurous cat, he jumped quickly over the rough wooden fence into a pristine garden. The garden had a pond with garden gnomes and a big wicker basket of cat treats. Cinder instantly pelted towards the basket, not noticing a man creeping up behind him, the basket lid in his hands...

No-one noticed anything strange about the man driving down the road. However, if you looked closely, you might notice the claw marks on the door. And you might hear the faint yowling and hissing coming from the back of the van. A man got out of the truck after parking outside a skyscraper in the city. He went in the lift up to the 39th floor, carrying a big wicker basket, firmly holding the lid on. Sometimes, however, it did seem to open a little on its own.

In the city there are lots of foxes and street rats, vicious creatures who attack anyone unlucky enough to be out alone at night. Trust me, you do not want to be anywhere near them, especially when they're in a bad mood. As soon as the man, Joshua, had entered his office, he opened the basket. Cinder immediately leapt out, heading for the door. Joshua slammed it shut, but not quick enough. Cinder bounded down the stairs. But Joshua took the lift, and arrived at the ground floor first, and prepared himself to catch the runaway cat.

It took a lot of struggling for Cinder to realise that he could just drop out of Joshua's arms... he pelted out the door and ran all the way home. Perhaps no-one will ever know why Joshua wanted to trap a cat, or why Cinder disappeared in the first place... Eventually, perhaps, somebody will find out!

A Black Cat's Story
By Aamina

My life has always been hard. Being a black cat in 1876 is dangerous. There are very superstitious people around now. Us black cats are believed to belong to witches and carry curses. No-one has ever loved me. I was born on the rocky streets by old London. Only to be kicked and hurt. I wasn't even given a name. If I could have one I would say Sarah or maybe Ellie. This is my story.

The earliest memory I have is when my mum abandoned me at one month old. She took me down an alley and then ran away. I found a soaked, squishy cardboard box and I nestled in that and drifted off into a long sleep. Waking up, I remembered I was in that dingy, disgusting alley. Summoning all my strength, I crawled out into the blazing light. I was young and foolish and thought anyone would love me. All I got were scowls and kicks and all types of words. Then I heard a small rumbling. My mother would always feed me, but today I had to find my own food.

I had been scavenging for many hours and finally found a big old bin behind the butcher's. In there, I found bits of meat, tuna, anything a cat could want. So I knew now where to find food.

Growing up, I became slick and fast. I had the stealth of a mouse. I had my own territory – even dogs wouldn't go there. At night, I slept under a blanket of stars. During the daytime, I got kicked, but it didn't really matter. I had almost everything I needed. Except for a loving family. One day, the merchants were shouting more than usual,

"The King will be touring London! Here comes the King!"

Creeping around, I just managed to get past the stampeding feet.

The next day, roads were closed and a beautiful golden carriage was being pulled by firm, strong horses. Maybe I could...

Looking around, I was scanning for any way to get into the carriage. I jumped up onto a rooftop and down into the carriage. I looked up. The King was an old man with a kindly sort of face. He had lots of wrinkles and looked down on me. I waited to be hurt...

Instead of hurting me, the King looked down

and smiled. Then he did something nobody had ever done before, he picked me up and settled me in his lap. Too surprised to move, I just sat still. Smiling, he said: "You will be living with me now, Ellie."

I had nothing for most of my life, and then – everything! A house, a name, an owner, and I was valued. After years of trying, somebody loved me.

Cat Wars

By Tor

Chapter 1 – The Journey Begins

Aboard the starship *The Purrseverance* our journey begins.

"How much longer?" Zephyr the cat asked.

"As you should know, we are exactly 4.546925476 light years away from our destination; as you should also know, I am completely unaware why we are heading there. You do know that only a few living beings have ever come out of this system alive?" the computer replied.

"Yes, I know, Computer, and when Zephyr asks for the time, can you just give it?" the last cat lord of the beam said.

"Of course, do forgive me, My Lord, and we should be dropping out of time warp in 3,2,1 and, here we are!" said the computer eagerly.

"Why are we here?" Zephyr asked.

"Zephyr, you should know why we are here – to infiltrate the pigeons. Computer! Delete what you just heard!" the lord said. "Let's land!"

"What about blasters?" Zephyr asked inquisitively. "I'll grab one."

"No, it's illegal here," the lord replied.

"No one will see it anyway, it's not legal for your laser to be here is it?" Zephyr replied, looking smug.

"Very well just don't use it," the lord said.

"Why are they here anyway, the empire?"

"I don't know," he responded. "Alright let's go."

The air was very dirty, and there was no one in sight, the only living things were distant shapes roaming the barren hills.

"We can't kill them, you know, these creatures. That's why, only birds are allowed to harm them," the last lord said.

After trekking for hours, on top of a hill they found a place where there were birds, pigeons to be exact, overlooking slaves mining in massive quarries.

"What is this? And why are they mining?" Zephyr asked.

"I think I know. Here, take a look through these goggles," the last lord of the beam said. "They're extracting something, I think, I am not sure what."

"I know, uranium, probably to power something, something big the rats made," Zephyr said calmly.

"Well there's the ship we can sneak on tonight, alright?" the lord said. "It will probably take us to Phoenixis, their home planet."

"Let's camp here, what do you say?" he asked.

Chapter 2 – On the Ship

As the two cats approached the warship under the cover of darkness they noticed their starship being taken on board.

"Well that sucks," Zephyr said.

"Yep, you got that right," the last lord of the beam said. "Look, there's a small hangar on the side – we can sneak in through that."

"Where's the ship?" Zephyr asked.

"In the main hangar probably," he said.

"I wonder what stuff they have in there," Zephyr said.

"Well, we're about to find out," the lord replied.

As the two approached the ship, little did they know that there was something on board that they never expected. After sneaking on through one of the side hangars they came across the computer room.

"Wow. What is this room?" Zephyr asked as they walked into the tall room.

"The computer room I think," the lord said.

"Can you hack into it?" Zephyr asked.

"Maybe, maybe not. I'll try to see what they're up to. K?" the lord said, turning round to see his friend on the floor before being knocked out himself.

Chapter 3 – The Cell

"What's going on?" Zephyr asked.

"Ah, you're awake. From what I understand, we are in a cell. We were captured in the computer room and are probably going to be interrogated soon," the lord said.

"Are there cameras here? Or microphones to listen to us?" Zephyr said worriedly.

"I don't think so, I have looked everywhere and it's just bare metal. Just follow my lead, ok?" the lord said.

"Ok," Zephyr replied. Just like the lord said, troopers came to get them for interrogation. So, before they reached the room they both lashed out, knocking out the troopers and escaping.

"Uh oh. The alarm has been raised!" Zephyr

shouted through all the alarms and red lights.

"Go down here!" the lord shouted, pointing with the stolen blaster down a suspicious hole.

"But..." Zephyr complained.

"Just do it, I'll follow you," he responded. So they jumped down into the trash compactor.

"What is this?" Zephyr asked.

"Trash compactor by the look of it," the lord said.

"So we get compacted and die," Zephyr said, sounding annoyed.

"No, we escape, because in case you didn't notice there's a door and all it needs is a shot from the blaster," the lord said, blasting the door open.

"Wow. Alright, where now?" Zephyr said as they stepped out into the empty hallway.

"The weapons room, so we can get our stuff back and something else," the lord said. "What's that?" he asked.

"You'll see," the lord replied, so they found themselves running through tunnels and hallways before eventually coming across the armoury. On every shelf there were blasters, machine blasters, explosives and weapons. There was one shelf labelled 'prisoners' items'

and on it there were blasters and the lord's laser.

"Here we go!" the lord said, chucking Zephyr a blaster and grabbing his laser.

"Alright let's go," Zephyr said.

"Wait, there's one more thing," the lord said with a smile.

Chapter 4 – Escaping with a Boom

The two cats ran through pillars, planting explosives before reaching the centre of the ship where thousands of rats were building a megastructure to destroy any planet which stood up to them.

"What is it?" Zephyr asked.

"I don't know but let's blow it up," the lord said.

"But what about the rats?" Zephyr asked.

"The rats can survive in space, so don't worry," the lord said.

"Ok; let's do it," Zephyr said. So off they went, planting explosive after explosive right under the empire's nose telling as many rats as possible what was going on, on the way. Everything went according to plan so after hours of planting and running they finally made it to the hangar.

"Look, there's our ship, how are we going to get there?" Zephyr said. "There's too many guards."

"We have explosives, don't forget, we can cause a distraction and escape," the lord said.

"Ok, let's do it," Zephyr said.

After placing the bomb, the cats rushed to a hiding place.

"How do we know it won't set everything off and kill everyone?" Zephyr asked.

"It's far away from everything else so don't worry," the lord said, and then BOOM – a massive explosion shook everything, and then another one, and then one more. Birds, confused, were running everywhere and flapping their wings frantically.

"I thought you said it wouldn't explode them all," Zephyr hissed.

"Well, was wrong, I guess. Let's go," the lord replied. Running in and out of explosions they found themselves in front of the ship. Rushing in, they rushed into the chairs. "Computer!" the lord shouted.

"Yes?" it responded calmly.

"Get us out of here! If you haven't noticed, this place is exploding!" the lord shouted again.

"Alright let's go!" the computer said gleefully just as the ground gave way. "Another adventure I wasn't part of! So, what did I miss?" it asked as the warship exploded behind them.

The Musical Cat
By Grace

There was a cat. Just a normal cat (as far as we know). His name was Harry. Every passing hour, he was gazing out over the streets of Kennington, from his warm cosy bed above the welcoming radiator. His kind, caring master was able to play the violin to a great standard. She was always working hard, teaching her students. Harry was mainly a black cat with a few hints of grey (since he was an old cat) apart from the large white patches on his back. He had sharp spotting eyes too.

Recently, the owner of Harry had adopted another cat named Rupert. And oh goodness was he a little trouble maker! Whenever there was a lesson, Harry would either be dozing off in his bed, or prowling around keeping an eye on Rupert.

Now, ever since he was a kitten, when he first discovered the violin, it was constantly in his mind that he might have the chance to investigate one properly. He loved to stare at the delicately carved scroll, the shining polished wood, the thin metal wires and the long horse hairs on the bow. Each day, he would sit listening to the melodic sounds the wonderful instrument had the ability to make.

Now, Harry had a massive secret. Harry could play the violin and he only found out a few days ago...

When he was outside, looking for some food, he ended up outside a charity shop. All of the donation bags were lined up against the wall outside. Shortly after that, a scruffy homeless person went through the bags and pulled out a warm snuggly sleeping bag and grinned with joy that they had something to sleep in. Harry did the same. He used his retracting claws to rip the bag. Eventually, he found an unusually shaped case... the case of a violin. The zips had already been pulled so the case was easy to open. Harry nudged the latch and let the case lid open.

It was all Harry had wanted. It had a reasonable choice of bow, some deluxe bow rosin, a new cloth, a shoulder rest, of course, the actual violin itself. He carefully put on the shoulder rest, put some rosin on the bow, just the way he saw his owner do it, got into position, and played. It was almost as if his paws had minds of their own, doing long notes, short notes, and even reaching the high notes.*

Harry was not the only one who could hear it though. Pedestrians walking across the roads, passers by and all sorts of other people were listening. They seemed to enjoy it and before Harry knew it, he was being showered with money! He was probably the first (if not best) violin-playing cat in the world. Harry was having the time of his life!

By the time Harry had made about £100, his fingers started to get weary. Shortly after that, a rather scary, mean looking man towered above him like a giraffe. As quick as a flash, the man sprang into the pile of cash and took a handful of it and dashed off into the distance. The rotter! Poor Harry, he had worked hard for that money! He wanted it back! He put the violin away and sprinted off to get his well-earned savings back. Right, left, down the stairs, right again, up the alley way and... into his master?!

"Oh, look guys, there is the cat violinist!" shouted someone who had just given Harry some money for his playing.

"So you're saying that my cat—"

"Yep!"

"That is the money he made that is being robbed."

"Why didn't someone call the police then!" exclaimed Harry's owner. She then pulled out her phone and dialled 999.

A few minutes after that, the police arrived. They used their special dogs to track down the man. They went along the cobbled paths. They eventually came to the man in a supermarket, buying some food.

"FREEZE, and stop right there!" they bellowed. "You are under arrest for the robbery of this poor cat's money!" They pulled out a pair of glimmering handcuffs and clipped the culprit together and threw him into the car. "Now you shouldn't be seeing him anymore," the policeman informed them.

And that's how it happened. His owner sadly didn't believe that poor Harry could play the violin to the high standard that people said that he could play.

The next day, Harry couldn't believe his eyes when he found the violin that he played the day before, untouched, exactly where he had left it. So he pulled it all the way home, through the catflap and hid it behind the sofa.

Every night, he would carefully pull out the case and practise outside very quietly.

Now, not only was Harry amazing at the violin, he had many mean, competitive rivals in the neighbourhood. There were Barry and Pixel, his two main rivals. One day, he was prowling along the paths in Kennington, and Barry sprang out of a laurel bush. He was a large ginger tabby cat with small blue eyes with huge pupils like swirling pools of endless darkness. He wanted his place back as king of the neighbourhood!

They both fought like bolts of lightning, zapping at each other furiously. They gave each other itchy wounds and ripped their skin. They fought both tooth and claw, biting, scratching, hitting, and squashing was all included. They were both worn out and decided to stop. They had not called a truce-YET.

The day after that, Harry found a letter from his best friend, a cat called Tabby. It was all in 'cat' so no one could understand. It read:

Miawwmiaww,
Moaw miooow nomm mamw maammmo
mom miaonm anom man wamon mawon
mano mamamwm miaom maws man

mammo wanno mawwno mallon mal monna malwn. Miannnnnnnmmmww, wamno.

Harry was delighted to read that. It had translated:

Dear Harry,

Barry told me that you had a fight yesterday. He told me to tell you that he is going to surrender as long as you call him the prince of this place.

A shaking of paws from Tabby.

Harry clearly thought that this meant he was now the king of the neighbourhood. And indeed he was! So he went back into his warm cosy house to count up the money he had made during the time he was playing. As he was doing this, he was thinking to himself when he should show his master just how well he could play and what if the whole world knew...

He pondered. Maybe he could join an orchestra, or play in the streets again, or become a teacher. Wait –no –that wouldn't work. It was all up in the air.

It was now winter and coming close to Christmas time and it was -1 degrees celsius and snowing. All of the children were playing in the snow and a young choir were singing mellow carols and all of the families were snuggling up by their fires, watching seasonal films and enjoying festive food. Harry's favourite part was the music!

This was Harry's chance to play. Surely there would be a Christmas music competition to play in. The question is, how was he going to enter, when he is a cat!? He had an excellent idea! Now, this is how he did it. Harry jumped down reluctantly from his warm snug bed. He gave a large meooooooooooooooooooowww and grabbed attention from his owner and carefully pulled out the violin case from behind the sofa – "Harry! You really can play the violin!" exclaimed his owner with a look of disbelief. Harry then jabbed his paw into the centre of an advertisement for a music competition and pointed at the violin section. He even pulled out the violin and put rosin on the bow and began to play a beautiful Christmas song.

His owner had no choice but to sign him up and let him play.

On the day, she drove him off to Abingdon to play. Harry was not the slightest bit nervous but he was very excited. When they got there, there were lots of other people there and Harry was put in a group with four other people and their names were Louie, Anne, Mary and Charlie and they all played the violin. After that, the judge asked them to come into a room where they could play.

"Right, I am to see which one of you can play the best today," said the judge. Everyone took their turns to play while the judge was listening to their playing. Then it was Harry's turn. He took a deep breath, and played. He was amazing! His fingers were going so fast!

After they had all played, the judge told them who won. "And the winner is...

LOUIE!!!!!!!" Harry was so disappointed that he wasn't the winner.

"No, hold on, I got that wrong. So actually Harry is the winner!" shouted the judge.

It was all over the news that day. Harry was now famous. He was now considered a professional violinist. The day after that, the Berlin Philharmonic Orchestra (the best one in the world) hired him and he did not accept because he wanted to be a normal cat again and king of the neighbourhood!

A Cat's Tail

By Georgia

In a beautiful village on a sweet road, lived a woman, her family and 2 cats. Over the years the woman's family grew old and left home, which left her with her 2 cats, and they all grew older too. A couple of years passed and one of her cats became ill and sadly passed away. Which left her with one cat called Timmy. Timmy was a fluffy, handsome tabby cat with sleek, white paws and a small, chocolate coloured nose and glistening emerald eyes.

Timmy didn't understand what happened to his cat companion, so to show his emotions he cried and meowed all day and night seeing if he would come back. The women got so fed up with Timmy's constant noise, so she decided to make him stay outside and not come in her warm house.

One crisp winter morning a kind, happy girl cycled passed and saw Timmy crying and shivering under a hydrangea with its leaves all fallen around it. The girl stopped her bike and carefully walked over to him. The girl tried to stroke him but he peered up to her and turned his head. His fur was all matted and hard, but that didn't stop her from checking on the cat every day. Every day he got less and less timid. Then she started to brush his cold, knotted fur. It took a long time for his fur to be shiny again, but that didn't stop him from crying.

One day, the girl was outside in the frosty weather crunching on the frosty grass.

The girl remembered and said "Oh no I need to go feed that cat!" As she quickly turned around to sprint to the house, he was there. Its like he just appeared. She sat down on her dewy, wet bench and he jumped up beside her. Whilst she was stroking him, she saw he had a collar on. That wasn't there before? The girl looked more deeply at it and saw it said 'TIMMY'. The girl was called in for her lunch so said goodbye to the cat and left.

Timmy saw she had left a crack of the door open which was just the right size for him. He slowly creeped up to the door to take a peek.

He silently stepped his paw though the door then carefully snuck into the house. The house was humongous to Timmy because he hasn't been in a house for ages. Scattered along the floor were by the looks of it dog toys. He never knew she had a dog. Then he came across to a room and quickly ran to it. He saw a massive bed, jumped onto it and got comfy. After a while Timmy heard thumping and banging. He shyly took a little look. A big, bulky black Labrador came in licking his slobbery mouth, after eating his lunch. He came to lay on his bed and saw Timmy. Timmy looked up and saw him! He got up as fast as he could and scurried off. He ran everywhere around the house. When he stopped, he waited around a corner.

Timmy checked everywhere to see where the dog was. Timmy felt a drop of cold drool on his head, he looked up to see the dog with its drooling mouth wide open ready to pounce on him. Timmy saw the door, it started to close, Timmy got worried. He jumped over the big dog and sprinted through a crack of the door and ran under the bench.

Just as Timmy got comfy again the girl came out from her lunch to see Timmy. Timmy felt calmer after a few strokes.

The girl sighed and said, "Hey Timmy I am sorry to say but I am going on holiday for a week." Timmy thought about this to himself.

Nothing was said. The day after she was packing for her holiday. Timmy waited and waited for her to come out. In the end she came out but only for a couple of warm strokes.

Sadly, the next day the girl was leaving for her trip, Timmy had a tremendous idea to sneak into the house. He rapidly ran out to her back door and dashed straight into the heavy glass. Timmy fell onto the floor dizzy. The door looked like it was closing so Timmy decided to do his trick again and silently creep into her toasty house.

Timmy was though the door and in her house, Timmy gazed around the tall house. "MEOWWW" they locked the door straight on him, what was he going to do he thought? Would they leave the door open for him? Then just as he got over the feeling of being locked in he heard rumbles and crunching. He could smell a disgusting odour. It was from the dog!!!

The dog plonked over to Timmy and said, "Hello I am Bosco!" in an excited voice. Timmy was confused why the dog was so nice to him after what they did to each other the last time they met.

Timmy calmly said "Oh, hello there I am Timmy." After that they became best friends.

A week later the girl came home from her hot, sunny holiday to the wet, cold weather back in her small village, to find Timmy in her house! He was sleeping snuggled against Bosco. The girl looked at them, and said, "Maybe he could stay with us," she said with a smirk. The next morning the girls' parents agreed about Timmy staying with them and they lived happily ever after!

(Based on a true story about me and my pets.)

Lost

By Alexandra Vetta

We're moving.

I turn around and watch my street disappear into the mist, but I don't turn away, even when we turn onto the motorway, I still stare at where my house used to be.

The three hour journey goes all too fast, and it feels like only moments had passed when my dad calls, "We're here!"

I take in the scene before me; a small house in the middle of a strange, polluted town. It's a mess. My parents though, seem to see some sort of paradise, as they unload the car smiling and moving their hands in elaborate motions, I don't know what they're saying, though because I still haven't moved, still haven't turned my head.

"Couldn't we have at least stayed for Christmas?" I complain as we start bringing suitcases into the house.

"Cheer up! It gives us a chance to make memories here, before you start school!"

School, I think, sudden panic rushing through me, I have to go to school here.

The twenty four hours leading up to Christmas day gives me time to distract me from all my worries about starting school in the city. Decorations are being rushed onto the portable, tiny tree and the boxes with all our furniture in are getting muddled with all the actual presents. The present I thought might be a new beanbag for me turned out to be one of the kitchen chairs.

Before I know it, it's Christmas Eve, and we're leaving treats out for Santa and his reindeer. Tonight, I'm probably the only child who can sleep. I'm not lying awake in anticipation, like I usually would. I feel like tomorrow is just any other day. The night passes quickly, and the morning comes. Christmas. It would be so much better at our old home.

I walk downstairs slowly, to see my parents waiting in the living room, with gifts. Despite myself, I can't help feeling a bit excited.

"Open this one first!" Mum pushes a large box in my direction.

I rip open the wrapping paper and strip the Sellotape sealing the box shut and then my hands freeze

"Is this real?" I ask shakily as a kitten noses its way out of the box.

All my parents do is smile, leading me to the conclusion that I'm not dreaming.

"Lucky." I lift the tiny thing up, hardly daring to breathe. "That's what I'm calling it."

After that, my life changed. It's amazing how a kitten can change your life. I think that this new house could be a home, if I gave it a chance and school is better than I thought

The Nasio Trust is a UK registered charity and Kenyan NGO which supports orphaned and vulnerable children and empowers communities in Kenya to break the cycle of poverty and thrive, by focusing on Education, Healthcare and Sustainable Livelihoods. As a grassroots charity we work in the heart of the community to identify and meet their needs.

We believe children should not grow up in institutions like orphanages, where they are isolated from society because of poverty, sickness, disease or death of parents. Children should live in a loving family with dignity without being stigmatised by the cause of their vulnerability.

View the website to see how you can help.

www.thenasiotrust.org

Profits from sales will help stock the first community library in Mumias, west Kenya.

Acknowledgments

Nancy Mudenyo Hunt and the Nasio Trust for building the first community library in the district of Mumias in west Kenya. *Cosmic Cats* will be its first book.

James Amori: The acting head teacher of Mumias Township Primary School for supporting the *Cosmic Cats* project.

Caroline Knighton: The head teacher of St Swithun's CE Primary School Kennington, Oxfordshire.

Lesley Maskell: Upper Junior Leader St. Swithun's CE Primary School.

Paul Gamble: Writer, naturalist and Kennington Parish Councillor.

and

Julia Golding: Novelist and screen writer.

for together selecting the stories from St Swithun's to be included in *Cosmic Cats*.

Alexandra Vetta: For writing a story to send to Mumias and her sisters **Antonia Vetta** and **Anastasia Vetta** for illustrating her story.

Korky Paul: Illustrator for designing the cover and being patron of the project

Wilbur: For endorsing it.

Faisa Turlubekov: For the front cover illustration

Andy Severn of Oxford eBooks: For typesetting, producing and publishing *Cosmic Cats*.